MORE THAN WORDS

REBEL BOOKS BOOK 2

SUSAN HARRIS

Originally published as Kindle Vella Episodes

Cover Design by: Gem Promotions
Typography by: Gem Promotions

PROLOGUE

Cliona

CLIONA COULD FEEL her heart beating hard inside her chest. She was the one who had suggested that she and the woman she'd been talking to online for the last six months finally shared a picture with one another, but now that it was finally happening, Cliona was nervous as hell.

Dani was her ideal woman; smart, funny, and loved music as much as Cliona did. Despite the fact that the conversations they had outside of the chatroom were just voice calls, Cliona had never felt like this about another woman. And despite the fact that Dani was living in London for work, Cliona was certain that they could somehow make a go of things.

- **Dani:** You change your mind?
- **Cliona:** No...just nervous...
- **Dani:** Me too.

Cliona didn't think that Dani had anything to be nervous about. When she laughed, it sounded like sin and seduction, so even before Cliona had ever seen a picture, Cliona knew that Dani was beautiful, inside and out. Cliona just had to take a leap of faith that this was meant to be.

Bringing up the picture that Cliona had selected to reveal herself to Dani, she swallowed hard as she pressed the send button, then waited anxiously while Dani typed a response.

- **Dani:** Damn, Cliona...You are gorgeous.

Heat flushed her cheeks as a smile curved her lips, as Cliona waited for Dani to send her a picture. Time ticked by as Cliona started to think that Dani wasn't going to send a picture back to her.

- **Cliona:** Dani? You still there?

Cliona watched as the dots for typing appeared on screen, then stopped, then started again after an agonising minute. She could understand that Dani was nervous, but after all the late-night conversations, all the deep and meaningful talks, did it really matter what they looked like?

- **Dani:** I don't want you to hate me...there is something I haven't told you about me.

Now, that made Cliona nervous, her heart sinking.

- **Cliona:** Well, you can be honest now.
- **Dani:** Please don't hate me...

Cliona went to reply, to tell Dani that nothing she could say could make Cliona hate her, that she was a little bit in love with her already when a picture appeared in the chat. And it was a face she knew well enough for anger to spike in her veins.

- **Cliona:** Is this some joke? After everything over the last 6 months and you wanna play catfish now? Sending me a pic of Danika Keane and thinking I wouldn't know who the hell she was? Any goddamn lesbian worth their salt knows who Danika is...I can't

```
believe I wasted my time on
you. Have a nice life, Dani,
if that's even your real
name.
```

Cliona closed the internet browser and immediately blocked the number that she had for Dani, before throwing it halfway across the room and letting the tears of anger and pain flow down her cheeks.

She should've known better to think that she could find love in a chatroom.

CHAPTER ONE

Cliona

FOUR WEEKS Later

Cliona sat in the middle of Rebel Books deliveries, trying to sort through the newest releases to put them on the shelves. As manager of the store, Cliona was responsible for a lot of things, but since Niamh Kent, her boss, and friend, had gotten entangled with a genuine rock god, Cliona had taken it upon herself to take over some of Niamh's responsibilities.

Niamh was just about the hit the last trimester of her pregnancy that had not only surprised Niamh and her boyfriend, Oli Scott, but the entire world when renowned bad boy Oli had settled down with the younger sister of Heartache Melody guitarist, Jameson Kent.

When after a hot summer day at the shop Niamh fainted, it was decided that they would hire more staff, and Niamh would take some well-deserved time to enjoy her pregnancy and her happy ending. Though Niamh had protested, Cliona, Nessa, and Sorcha, who was Niamh's business partner had all outvoted her, forcing Niamh to take a step back and let them handle all the heavy-duty stuff at the shop.

Cliona liked to keep Niamh involved by asking Niamh to help her out with selecting books to order, asking her for ideas for book displays, and things that Niamh could do without leaving her ridiculously beautiful new house that she shared with Oli.

Sundays were a normally quiet day at the bookshop, so Cliona took advantage of the stillness to go through the inventory. Molly, one of their new staff, a college student who worked weekends and the odd day here and there, was manning the till for any customers who might stroll in.

To be honest, Cliona had been only too happy to take on all the extra work so that it would take her mind off the shitshow that was her love life. The only person that knew what had happened to her with the catfish was Sorcha, who had noticed that Cliona wasn't herself. In the end, Cliona blurted out all the sordid details of her stupidity.

Sorcha had listened to her, then told her that she should just ask Niamh to ask Danika herself if she had been the one to actually be messaging her. Cliona had considered it. But after a week of moping, she decided that she was better off not having confirmation that she'd been a fool. It didn't matter that Oli and the real Danika Keane were best friends. It would confirm to Cliona that the Dani she had been duped by was nothing more than a catfish. Cliona didn't want everyone to know that she had been so eager to fall in love that she'd been made a fool of.

Cliona knew Niamh would never make her feel like she had been stupid, their friendship solid since the day that they had met. It was months before Rebel Books had opened when Cliona had gone for a job interview fresh from her business management course. It had felt more like a chat than an interview. Even though she had only applied for the assistant manager's job, Niamh and Sorcha had offered her the manager's job before the interview was over.

Apparently telling Niamh that she was a massive Laurell K. Hamilton fan was what won her over.

Cliona had been delighted to stumble upon people who accepted her for who she was. Growing up, Cliona had not felt like she could be herself in her conservative Catholic school, had not felt like the girls in her year would understand the fact that while they all fancied boys, Cliona had known that she liked girls.

Her parents had never accepted the fact that she was a lesbian. They were both overtly religious. To

7

them being gay was a sin. They seemed to forget that Cliona was exactly the same daughter that they had loved for sixteen years, seeing only this thing that didn't fit with their belief system.

Cliona had been a late addition to her family, her mother falling pregnant at thirty-nine after her older brothers had already been raised. Simon and Eoghan were now in their forties, both living on opposite sides of the world. Simon in the US and Eoghan in Abu Dhabi. They had their own lives and families, and while Cliona kept in contact with them, the gap in age had been too vast.

But for three years when Cliona had come out, before Simon had gotten a job in the US, he and his wife had opened their home to her, and even asked her to come to the US with them. Cliona had just gotten into the management course she wanted and had been still a little optimistic that her parents would come round and see that their daughter wasn't tainted by the devil with sinful urges.

And Cliona wasn't even being dramatic.

Now in their sixties, her parents hadn't seen her in like five years, though she knew from her last conversation with her brothers that they were both still preaching the good word of the Lord, and very proud of both their sons. Cliona supposed that her brothers were lucky that their parents didn't like social media or they would know that her nephew, who was attending a very respectful law school and in a very happy relationship with his very male partner.

Simon had been happy for her to stay in the house that he had lived in with his wife, had even helped her with a rent-to-buy scheme. Cliona had finally managed to secure a mortgage after a hard slog of saving. Niamh paid her well for all that she did and not many people her age were lucky enough to own their own home in their mid-twenties.

Cliona hated to admit that she missed the noise and the chaos of living with other people. The house was sometimes too quiet. Her house never felt like a home, buried under the weight of expectations, of the fear of being rejected, and having to hide the things she liked in order to please her parents.

It was why she couldn't decide on how to decorate her house, to make the house that was once her brother's feel like hers. Part of her wanted to indulge teenage Cliona, paint the walls black, and hang pictures of Gwen Stefani, Amy Lee, Joan Jett, and all the other musicians she loved and been forced to hide from her parents.

The only thing that Cliona was certain of was that she wanted a wall of bookcases that would make all the bookstagrammers and TikTokers green with envy.

Smiling, she unboxed a delivery of signed books that Cliona had ordered from CTP Publishing. Cliona and Niamh had read a few titles from their catalogue after a customer came in asking about a book by a local author and decided to order some copies. It had been Cliona's idea to message the publisher and ask about some signed copies. It turned out that the owner, Veronica, was a big fan of Oli's and was only too happy to send some autographed copies to the woman who was dating him.

Setting aside one of the complete sets of Julie Wetzel's Kindling Flames series for Niamh because she was a fan of the series, and then making sure she kept the copies of Alternate Academy by Melissa Woods, the brand-new YA that wasn't releasing for another few weeks but was sure to be a hit. Veronica had been very generous in sending them the book early, so it would be on Rebel Books shelves on release day.

Cliona kept sorting until morning turned to after-noon, and the only thing left to do was to put the books on the shelves. Getting to her feet, Cliona stretched out her limbs, stopping to get herself a tea before getting back to work. Once all the books were on the shelves, Cliona took a step back and admired her work.

When she had a few days off next week, Cliona decided that she would make a start on the bookcases she'd ordered weeks ago and didn't have the time to put together. After the last few weeks of heartbreak and moping, Cliona needed to put herself back on track and start to get on with her life. To stop dwelling on things that Cliona had no control over.

And while making up some bookcases and picking

a paint colour for walls might not be much to most, it was a step in the right direction for Cliona. She needed to stop thinking about Dani, about her parents, and concentrate on moving forward with her life. She had to be open to the chance that better things were coming for her and stop thinking about a woman who wasn't even real.

Chapter Two

Cliona

Cliona was about to finish up for the evening. As she waited for Nessa to show up, Cliona perched herself on the stool behind the till and leafed through a music magazine. When she stumbled upon an article about the real Danika Keane, Cliona found herself staring at the picture of the drop-dead gorgeous rockstar for longer than she should.

Chiding herself for being an idiot, Cliona closed the magazine with a huff. The door to Rebel Books opened, and Niamh Kent walked in. Cliona had always thought that Niamh was beautiful, but in the years that Niamh had been dating her ex Brian, the curvy, smiling, Niamh had faded away, leaving her friend self-conscious, and a shell of who she was.

Cliona, Sorcha, and Nessa had all watched as

Niamh slowly emerged from the ugliness of her relationship with Brian, and then Oli Scott had come in and swept Niamh off her feet. Gone was the cautious look in her eyes as if she was afraid of doing or saying something wrong, replaced with eyes that now shimmered with light which made her beautiful to look at.

Even now as she proudly wore a t-shirt with her brother's band's logo on it and a very big bump, her brunette hair hung in loose waves and her smile was wide, with a protective hand on her belly. Cliona darted to her feet, ready to ask Niamh what the hell she was doing here when her friend held up her hand, halting Cliona.

"Before you give out to me for showing up, Oli dropped me to the door before he went over to Rebel Ink, and my very handsome goth rocker will swing by and get me once he finishes talking to his tattoo husband."

Cliona barked out a laugh as Niamh walked over to the seating area and lowered herself down into the seat. Taking the seat beside her, Cliona asked Niamh did she want anything to drink, but Niamh shook her head.

"Thanks, but at the moment, any time I dare drink something I almost immediately need to pee." Niamh rubbed her belly. "Mini Scott in here likes to give mammy's kidneys a good hiding, especially at stupid o'clock in the morning. And then it's all the weird cravings. I had bacon and ice cream for breakfast this morning."

Cilona chuckled, running a hand through her hair. "When you say mini Scott, have you and Oli decided to find out what ye are having? I bet Oli is impatiently trying to figure it out."

This time, it was Niamh that laughed, "Actually, no. Oli is all for the element of surprise. It's me that keeps pestering him to find out. I might have bitten his head off when we went looking at buggies and they had this one I liked but it only came in blue and pink. He calmly smiled at me in that sexy way he does and said that it didn't matter if it was a boy or a girl, once it was healthy and happy."

"Did you go all goo eyed at him and go aww?" Cliona asked as Nessa came in and went to put her things away before joining them.

Niamh's cheeks went a shade of crimson as she chewed on her bottom lip. "No. I burst into tears inside the shop, telling Oli I was gonna be a terrible mother and I should have been thinking the same as him."

Nessa came over and sat down beside them, as Cliona said. "I bet Oli just wrapped his arm around you and kissed you and then you forget all about your haywire hormones." Niamh's cheeks went a darker shade of red and Cliona lifted her brows.

"Or did you find a more productive avenue for your hormones?"

Niamh covered her face in her hands as both Cliona and Nessa laughed.

"Stop it!" Niamh groaned, peeking out through her fingers. "Oli was always sexy as sin but lately, it doesn't matter if he's writing a song or washing the dishes, I just want to strip him naked and have my way with him. But that is enough about my sex life and let's start talking about more suitable Sunday conversations."

They chatted for a few minutes, Cliona catching Niamh up on some work stuff just to keep Niamh mollified, then Nessa told them that her landlord was selling up and she needed to look for somewhere else to live before she got up to ring up a sale for a customer.

Niamh looked at Cliona with a worried expression. Nessa didn't talk much about her past, but the younger woman had been through far more than anyone knew. They were aware of why she worked the night shift, and they were happy to accommodate her. But now that she was being evicted, that was a worry the poor woman didn't need.

"Why don't you let Nessa move in upstairs?"

Niamh tilted her head. "Into my apartment?"

Cliona rolled her eyes with a sigh. "You mean the apartment that you haven't been in since it took too much effort to walk up the stairs? Or since your ridiculously rich rockstar boyfriend bought a mansion for you and mini Scott. It would be the perfect solution for Nessa."

Niamh was grinning by the time Nessa came back over. Niamh asked her if she would move into the apartment above the bookstore, Nessa looked taken aback when Niamh mentioned it and they both watched as Nessa got visibly defensive.

Leaning back in her chair, Niamh rested her hands on her stomach. "It just dawned on me when you said you'd have to move out that upstairs would be perfect for you. I had just been telling Cliona I was thinking of letting it out and it's like everything lined up."

"I'm not a charity case, Niamh," Nessa said quietly, her lips pressed firmly together after speaking.

Niamh reached over and took Cliona's hand. "I know that. And we can talk about rent if it makes you happy, but considering you'd be upstairs, it's like you are taking on extra responsibility so the rent would be manageable. And you can totally do it up whatever way you like it."

Nessa still didn't look convinced, but she didn't have any time to argue as the door to the bookshop opened, and in sauntered genuine rock royalty. Oli Scott grinned as he spotted them all sitting down, his stride easy and confident.

"Ladies, what I miss?"

Nessa blushed as Niamh got to her feet. "Nessa was just considering whether or not to move in upstairs."

Oli placed a hand on the nape of Niamh's neck as he looked over at Nessa. "I think that's a grand idea.

Let me know when you need help moving and I'll grab one or two of the Rebel Ink lads to help ya. I'll get Gus to get some of his lads to hook you up with some new security like we got at the house."

"I don't want to cause any hassle."

Niamh rested her hand on Nessa's shoulder. "Believe me, it's no hassle. Oli's been bugging me about updating all the security at the shop and the apartment is part of it. And I'd much prefer to have family living in the place that gave me back my independence than some randomer. Think about it and let me know. Right now, I am starving, and my lovely boyfriend is going to take me somewhere I can get something nice and unhealthy."

Oli kissed her cheek, and in his eyes, Cliona could see just how much Oli adored Niamh.

"Your wish is my command, gorgeous. Ladies come over to the house any day or night next week and Niamh can show you the nursery. Me and Jameson did a great job."

The couple left a few minutes later, and Cliona chatted for a few minutes before she left Nessa to her thoughts, knowing that the other woman would need time to consider what it was that she was going to do about moving in upstairs.

She stopped off at her local Chinese takeaway before heading home. The silence in the house almost deafening until she turned on a random show and slumped down on her couch as she ate her food and glanced at her laptop. Cliona told herself that she didn't miss the faker who couldn't be honest with her about who she was.

Thankfully, even though Cliona didn't know what 'Dani' looked like, and since she was in London, there was no chance of her bumping into her, or looking at other women and wondering if they were the catfish she had told some of her deepest, darkest truths to.

Cliona needed to forget all about the mysterious internet catfish, and start looking at real people. She wanted someone to look at her the way Oli and Niamh looked at each other. Rolling her eyes at herself, Cliona didn't think she'd ever find someone to love her like that, and she was better off just accepting the fact.

CHAPTER THREE

Danika

DANIKA HAD FORGOTTEN how fucking green Ireland was.

She was used to the concrete and bustle of London, where people moved about and never really gave one another eye contact, everyone too busy to give anyone else the time of day. But in Ireland, where Danika had been born and mostly raised, people always had a friendly smile to greet you, and even if you were super famous, they never felt like they should interrupt you.

Even now, as she disembarked her flight from London to Cork, she caught people looking at her, then glancing away before whispering to their friends. Danika winked at the customs officer as he cleared her. Having gone through security, Danika posed for a few pictures and signed some autographs, asking the fans to wait to post because she was here to surprise a few people.

Oli Scott was her brother from another mother, her ride or die. When Danika's mam had enrolled her in the elite boarding school, the elite all-male boarding school along with Oli, he had kept her safe. They'd shared a room together with a soon-to-be movie star who happened to be very shy, to begin with.

Not that Oli had been as outrageously confident back then. It had been Danika who had been the one to lead them all astray and into mischief. It had been the three of them against the world, even after Oli had secured his record deal, he made sure that she and JJ were looked after. Hell, he'd even helped Danika land her own record deal a year after he had signed his.

All JJ had ever wanted was to act, had gotten an agent who, like what happened with Oli, had told JJ that in order for him to even be considered a leading man, he had to change who he was. Only JJ's closest friends and family knew that he was gay, and Danika had seen how lonely it had made her friend.

Her own loneliness had hit her even harder while she was staying in JJ's big country estate while Oli was recovering from his throat surgery. Seeing Niamh and Oli all in fucking loved-up bliss had made Danika pine. Jesus and now that made her sound like a massive bitch.

Danika was thrilled for Oli that he had found

Niamh and was on the verge of having the happy family her friend has always wanted. Oli's dad was a massive prick, and his poor mam had been in and out of the real world since Danika had known her. Danika's mam and Oli's mam had been part of an eighties pop band and her mam embarked on a career working on cruise ships after the band had faded away.

When Oli and Niamh had gone to bed one night, her and JJ sat on the couch, JJ with a wistful look on his face. he felt Danika's stare on him, had cast her a whole lot of side eye before he had drawled. *"Why are you staring at me?"*

"You're just so handsome I can't help myself. Such a shame we're gay."

JJ chuckled as he rolled his eyes. "Darling, even if we both fancied each other, I think you'd give me grey hairs and I haven't reached my George Clooney phase of my career just yet."

Danika barked out a laugh, then patted JJ on the leg. "He's besotted with her."

"He deserves it," JJ answered, lifting his beer to his lips before speaking again. "I had my parents, and you had your mum, scatty as she is. But Oli only had Arthur and we both know that man wasn't a good father. We should have known when he hired Manny and stopped the partying that he was angling to settle down. I've only known her a few days, but Niamh fits our Oli, the boy with the squint and the acne."

She had heard the loneliness in JJ's voice and how

it mirrored her own. Danika had not the best track record with relationships. Women loved the idea of Danika; the goth rock princess who swore like a sailor and was messy and slightly neurotic. But the reality of messy and neurotic wore off when Danika didn't answer her phone for days because a song had just consumed her. They didn't get that the Danika who screamed fuck you to the patriarchy in her music, was not all about the lavish parties and wild nights anymore.

Music was her first love and that was what consumed her with a vengeance.

But when she went on the music chat as Dani, she had been doing it only to talk to people about music and nothing else. She'd been chatting in there for a bit, then she had seen a comment Cliona had posted on a thread and decided to take a gamble, send her a message. Cliona had been hesitant to start, but soon they talked all the time, and Danika found that she missed Cliona when they didn't talk.

Of course, there had been this massive lie hanging over them. Danika wasn't sure that Cliona would feel the same about her when she revealed her true identity, but feelings had been caught, and it was time for her to just rip off the motherfucking plaster.

Danika had not been prepared for the angry outburst that followed.

Is this some joke? After everything over the last 6 months and you wanna play catfish now? Sending me a pic of Danika Keane and thinking I wouldn't know who the hell she was? Any goddamn lesbian worth their salt knows who Danika is...I can't believe I wasted my time on you. Have a nice life, Dani, if that's even your real name.

Cliona had vanished from the chatroom, had blocked her number, not knowing that the number Danika had given her was her *actual* phone number. All Danika had was a location in Cork, her first name, and that was it. She'd almost given up hope of finding Cliona and explaining to her that she was who she said she was, when Danika had checked the socials of Rebel Books, and seen a picture of the beautiful woman next to Niamh. She nearly dropped her phone when she realized that the Cliona she had been talking to was the same Cliona who managed Rebel Books for Niamh.

Ireland really was a fucking small place.

And that was what had spurred Danika to lead her security on a merry dance as she slipped out of her penthouse apartment, taking public transport to the airport, and then a budget airline flight she'd booked last night on a whim. Even her record label had no clue about her impromptu visit to Ireland. She had unfinished business with a certain lesbian.

Ducking into the bathrooms, Danika pulled off the baseball cap and looked at herself in the mirror. Her face had only the basic level of makeup, her off-day stuff where she wasn't all gothy. Even her clothes could be described as bland compared to some of the stuff she wore, however, it was needed in order to get around without too much fuss.

Danika dug into her bag for her platinum blonde wig. She hated when she had to go incognito and wear a wig. To put them on properly, it took patience and that was a skill Danika had always lacked. The movies had it all wrong with how quickly a wig went on and came off, but Danika knew sometimes it was a necessary evil.

She still hated wearing one though. Things fucking itched and made her look stupid.

Once the wig was not so professionally put on, and wearing her baseball cap, Danika went out and grabbed her suitcase off the carousel and was amazed that she managed to get passed some people who had gathered outside, went to the car rental desk and was out the door a few minutes later.

Having driven to Oli and Niamh's house, Danika grinned as she pulled her rental car up to Oli's security gate and pressed the buzzer, holding up her middle finger to the camera with a grin. The gate creaked open, and Danika eased the car in parked it, then jumped out and grabbed her bag.

The front door opened and her brother from another mother leaned in the doorway. Tall and lean with inked skin and a wicked smile, Oli had been her best friend since they were toddlers and she was delighted that he'd found his happy ending with a woman he was crazy for.

"What are you doing here, Dani?" Oli asked, his tone suspicious in a familiar way that made her laugh as she strode up and lifted her chin up to look at him.

"Can we get to the quizzing after you've shown me around the house? And I need to get this wig off me. The bitch is gripping my head like I owe it money."

CHAPTER FOUR

Cliona

CLIONA HAD MADE sure to set up a table on the main shop level to save Niamh having to traipse downstairs where they usually had their staff meetings. Niamh wouldn't have minded, but Cliona wanted to make it as easy as possible for her to feel comfortable. Oli had texted Cliona early that morning to say that Niamh hadn't slept very well but was adamant that she was attending the meeting.

It must be nice, right? Having someone looking out for you like that...

Niamh and Nessa were currently in Niamh's office after the other woman asked Niamh if she could speak to her the moment Niamh had arrived. Sorcha was the last to arrive, bursting in the door with a big smile. Cliona originally thought that Sorcha was just very bouncy and perky, but once she had gotten to know her, Cliona knew behind the girl next door beauty was a sharp intelligence and a quick wit.

The door to Niamh's office opened. Nessa came out and Cliona could see the relief on the other woman's face. Nessa had been stressing about Niamh's offer to take over the apartment above the bookstore, not wanting to take advantage, but Cliona knew that was the last thing Nessa would do. Nessa was as part of their Rebel Books family as everyone else, though there were still some secrets that Nessa kept to herself. That one definitely had some shadows that chased her.

Niamh followed Nessa out, a hand on her stomach as she winced, waving off Nessa when she started showing concern. Cliona gave Nessa a quick look, then hurried over to steer Niamh over to the seating area, making sure she was sat down in the comfiest chair and distracted her by asking her how her chat with Nessa went.

Arching a brow, Niamh glared at her. "I know what you lot are doing. Did Oli message and tell you that I had a shit night? He worries too much."

"Would you believe me if I said no?" Cliona asked with an exaggerated shrug that made Niamh laugh.

"Idiots. I'm fine. Mini Scott is fine. Nessa has agreed to move in upstairs. Life is fantastic." Niamh's voice elevated at the end of her sentence and Cliona could see how genuinely happy her friend was.

Sorcha and Nessa came over with drinks and they

got down to the business side of things. Niamh wanted them to hire a temporary manager to help Cliona while she was on maternity leave, and Cliona was adamant that they could cope with the added work-load without having to add anyone new.

"It's not like I have anything else to be doing with my time." Cliona said, surprised at how bitter her words sounded.

"Still, the three of you can't be expected to do everything I do and cover any absences. At least if you bring in someone else, Cliona can take over most of what I do. You do it anyway, Cliona, have been for ages now."

That was true, to be fair. When Brian had dumped Niamh, she'd been in a spiral and Cliona had jumped into help where Sorcha and Nessa couldn't. It was easy enough work for her to do, and she actually enjoyed it.

Leaning back in her seat, Cliona, folded her arms across her chest and listened to the back and forth from the women as they discussed baby names, and it was only when Cliona heard mention of Danika's name that she paid attention.

"It hadn't even occurred to me yet about having Mini Scott christened but Oli was sitting down in front of the piano the other day and he asked me if I wanted to do the whole church and holy water thing and Godparents."

"And what did you say?" Sorcha asked as she leaned over to grab a cookie.

"After I stared at him for a few minutes and he gave me a strange look, I said that I would like to have Godparents for Mini Scott. So maybe a Christening would be good."

"Oh my God," Sorcha gushed, causing them all to look at the blonde-haired woman. "How ever will I choose an uber rich godparent for my already uber rich baby. Talk about spoiled for choice, I mean, the goth princess or the movie star hunk for Oli, and then Niamh, you have your own rockstar brother to choose from. The kid is gonna have some epic fucking birthdays."

They all laughed as Niamh grabbed a biscuit and nibbled on it. "That's nearly word for word what Oli said after he asked me if I would be asking Jameson to be godfather."

A slow smile curved Niamh's lips as Cliona leaned forward. "I guess that smile means you're gonna ask Jameson?"

It wasn't that hard to know why Niamh would ask her brother. They had a very special bond, forged in grief for the girl they had both lost, and loved, in different ways. A loss like that had only strengthened their relationship. Cliona had always been so envious of that.

"Of course. Oli said it was good because he was going to ask Danika. Even if JJ got pissed off with him." A faint blush darkened Niamh's cheeks that normally meant she was thinking of her rockstar.

"And?" Cliona pushed for Niamh to spill more details.

"I asked Oli if it would hurt JJ's feelings, and Oli gave me that smile of his, turned back to the piano and said; Nah, I'll just tell him that he gets dibs on the second one."

Jesus, Niamh hadn't popped out one baby yet and Oli was planning on knocking her up again. When Cliona told Niamh that, she laughed, then ran a hand over her stomach. "Well, we do have a big house with plenty of spare rooms, so I'm not opposed to more mini Scotts."

They went back to talking about some more work stuff, with Sorcha delighted to tell them that some of the most recent promo from Oli and the Heartache Melody members had upped their online sales and they had made a tidy profit that Niamh and Sorcha wanted to put back into the business and for everyone to start thinking of ideas.

Niamh's phone chimed, a goofy smile on her face as she said. "It's Oli. He's on his way to collect me, says he has a surprise for me. I bet it's a new tattoo idea. Did you know he wanted to get some older ink laser removed so that he could get new tattoos? That man is insane sometimes."

Having to force Niamh to stay sitting down, the rest of them cleared up, until Cliona brought some books over for Niamh to take home to read and relax with. The door to Rebel Books opened. Cliona glanced over her shoulder, and her heart stopped.

Oli Scott strode in wearing a hoodie and jeans but looking every bit the handsome rockstar. But it wasn't Oli that had made her heart splutter. It was the gorgeous woman standing beside him.

Long black hair hung down around her in a way that made Cliona was sink her fingers into it as she pulled her close for a kiss, her full lips wore a sexy smile. Dressed in baggy jeans and a vest top, a hoody worn over it, but draped off her shoulders; Danika Keane was as breathtaking in person, as she was on TV and in music videos.

"Danika!" Niamh exclaimed as the other woman came over and gave Niamh a warm hug. "What are you doing here?"

With a snort, Danika glanced at Oli. "See, when Niamh's asks me that, it sounds way nicer."

Oli flipped her off, then came over to press a kiss to Niamh's lips, then helped her to her feet. "That's because Niamh doesn't know that you dodged your security, caused a mini heart attack to your label when you vanished, and then your best friend when you showed up on his doorstep without a word."

"It's called a surprise, fucker."

"It's called common courtesy, you decrepit old bitch."

Everyone was looking from Oli to Danika, but Cliona only had eyes for Danika. Piercing blue eyes turned in Cliona's direction, and for a stupid moment, Cliona thought she saw recognition in Danika's eyes.

"Oh Danika, let me introduce you to the girls. This is Cliona."

The world seemed to fall out from under Cliona's feet as Danika tilted her head to the side, and flashed Cliona a grin, "Oh I know who Cliona is. We're old friends."

Cliona had to have heard that wrong, right?

Her heart was beating like a drum as Danika's eyes danced, and Cliona knew that this was real. The catfish she had been talking to really was actually Danika Keane...

All these months of thinking that she had been made a fool of to find out that the woman she had been talking to, the woman she had been developing feelings for, was the sexiest woman alive. Cliona's eyes went wide as she saw the smugness in Danika's gaze, and heard the taunt in her tone as she said, "Hey Cliona, it's nice to finally meet you in person."

CHAPTER FIVE

Danika

DANIKA'S STOMACH dropped when she saw the look of shock on Cliona's face, aware that everyone had curious eyes on them. Although Oli was aware of what happened with Danika and her online relationship, he had no idea that it was Cliona, Niamh's friend, that Danika had been talking to. It was Oli who had said that he needed to go collect Niamh at Rebel Books, and Danika had been eager to tag along and hopefully lay eyes on Cliona in the flesh for the first time.

Cliona's mouth was still hanging open, as she fumbled to take her phone out of her very nice-fitting jeans and pressed dial. Not a second later, Danika's personal phone vibrated in her pocket and she took it out, holding up the caller idea for Cliona to see her name pop up on the screen.

"Jesus, she gave you her real number and not the fake number she tends to give people."

That seemed to startle Cliona, who took a step back and had yet to speak directly to Danika. In fact, she looked like a deer caught in the headlights, and the other women were starting to notice.

"Does someone want to fill the rest of us in on what the fuck is going on here?" asked the stunning blonde woman who was glaring at Danika like she'd just admitted a murder.

Danika arched her brow at Cliona, whose mouth closed then opened, then closed again, so Danika took it upon herself to explain to the others what was going on.

"Cliona and me, we've have been taking online for months and when I told her who I was, she accused me of lying and what was it, you said? *Sending me a pic of Danika Keane and thinking I wouldn't know who the hell she was? Any goddamn lesbian worth their salt knows who Danika is...I can't believe I wasted my time on you. Have a nice life, Dani, if that's even your real name.*"

Soft brown eyes widened in surprise at the realisation that Danika had memorized the entire conversation. Danika's heart squeezed, as the emotions of Cliona's rejection came tumbling back and Danika, like she tended to do, went into defense bitch mode.

"I've spent the last month expecting Nev and Kamie to slide into my DM's or show up at my door for an episode of *Catfish* after that. Or I guess that goddamn six months we spent talking didn't fucking matter when you thought I was bullshitting you."

There was no way to mask the venom and bitterness in her tone, but Danika was delighted to see a flash of heat in Cliona's gaze as she spoke the first words to Danika since she arrived.

"How the hell was I to know that Danika Keane was slumming it in a music chatroom and not living it large out with and different woman every night? How the hell was I to even know that you were real and not some wannabe messing with people's heads? Don't come to my workplace and get all pissy with me about this. Just don't."

Shit, maybe Danika had gone too far with showing up like this and just getting in Cliona's face? Oli and JJ always said that when she got something in her head, she was like a bull in a China shop, reacting rather than formulating a plan. Considering she had decided to hop on a plane and come to Cork on a whim during a sleepless night, then evaded her security, and turned off her work phone, they might be right.

But Danika Keane did not back down in an argument, even if she was wrong.

"Well, considering you blocked my number and didn't come back to the chatroom, how else was I gonna get you to talk to me? If you knew that I was coming here, would you have been MIA before I arrived? Or was it that as soon as you realized that I might be real, it scared the shit out of you, and you freaked the fuck out?"

Danika was aware that the level of her voice had risen so much that Oli had reached out and put a hand on her arm. Niamh had moved to stand beside Cliona, a frown on her face, as did the blonde and the other woman who looked like she wanted to be anywhere but stuck in between the two arguing women.

"Take it down a notch, Dani," Oli said softly, but his tone held an edge to it that was familiar to her, because, despite his public persona, Oli had very much been the voice of reason when they were teens.

It was the way Oli said her name, the shortened version of Dani that drew a shocked gasp from Cliona, and Danika couldn't help herself when she said. "I gave you the name my brothers call me. So ya, I didn't lie about that either. There's only a handful of people who get to call me that."

A hand squeezed her arm, and she glanced over her shoulder at Oli. Her best friend's face held the edge of a warning that Danika was pushing too hard. Of course, she was. The rejection from Cliona had hit her harder than Danika had expected.

When Danika had first made waves in the music world, being out and loud about it had meant a hell of a lot of women wanted to get in her bed. Her relationships burned bright and fast. Women grew tired of her quickly when the fantasy wore off or Danika said something that sent them packing. She'd been hurt before, and it had always seemed like it was easier to cut and run than face the inevitable heartache.

But Danika hadn't wanted to cut and run with Cliona.

Lifting her eyes to clash with Cliona's, Danika raised her eyebrows as if to say, balls in your court now, sweetheart. Cliona continued to stare at her but refused to utter another syllable. The air was thick with the tension of it all.

Niamh cleared her throat, and Cliona jerked her eyes downward.

"Maybe we should all just take a beat, let tempers dampen and then you two can have a chat when it's not all so raw and somewhere much less public."

Danika almost laughed because as much as Niamh and Oli were fretting about becoming parents, Niamh seemed to have her mammy tone down pat. Cliona seemed to bristle at her words, but she just turned on her heels and headed off into one of the offices, closing the door with a loud bang that told Danika all she needed to know about how pissed off Cliona was.

"I'll go talk to her," Niamh said as she rested a hand on her rounded belly, winced, and sucked in some air.

Oli was over next to her a second later, his own tattooed hand falling on her stomach. "You okay?"

Niamh smiled at Oli, though even Danika could see that she was in pain, "All good. Kicking up a storm is Mini Scott."

Danika saw something flash across Oli's face before it was gone, and Danika filed it away to bring up with Oli when they were alone again. Letting out a sigh, Danika looked toward the office Cliona had vanished through, then looked back at the assembled people.

"You stay there so Mini Scott doesn't decide to follow in their dad's footsteps and make a spectacular entrance before you are ready, and I'll go talk to Cliona. My mess, I'll clean it up."

Danika had taken a few strides forward when she heard Oli say her name. looking back at her friend, she held his gaze as he said. "Take it easy. Don't bulldoze your way in."

Rolling her eyes, Danika didn't bother giving Oli the middle finger because he was just reminding her that not everything in life required her full-on attitude. Her first face-to-face with Cliona hadn't exactly gone the way she had wanted it to, but then again, what had Danika expected Cliona to do when confronted with the truth?

Had Danika really expected her to close the distance between them, take her face in her hands, and kiss her with lips that Danika had been dreaming about kissing even before she had even seen a picture of the woman who had consumed Danika's life for six months?

Well, a girl could hold out hope, right? After all, that's how it always happened in the movies.

Taking a beat to roll back the hostility and try

another angle when attempting to talk to Cliona again. Oli was right when he told her to take it easy. If she wanted any chance in hell that Cliona might give her a shot for real, then she couldn't get all huffy about how their online chats had ended.

Steeling herself against the possibility that Cliona would no longer want a bar of her, Danika raised her fist and knocked gently on the door to the office.

Chapter Six

Cliona

Cliona had never felt so embarrassed in her entire life.

Not that she had been so utterly wrong about the fact that she had been talking all along with Danika bloody Keane, but that Danika had shown up at her place of work and just ripped into her. Cliona had been so mesmerised by just how mind-numbingly beautiful Danika was.

Sleek black hair that was pulled back gave Cliona the full effect of Danika's face. Pale blue eyes against an ivory skin tone and full lips that were red, as if they had been kissed all night. Her skin was the same ivory shade as the skin that was on show, a stark contrast with the black lace of the bra that peeked out from her tank top. Her lower half was encased in a pair of leggings that seemed moulded to her skin, making her already dangerous curves invite Cliona's touch.

It had been that horrendous thought that had sent Cliona running for the safety of her office. Because the Dani she had feelings for was the Danika Keane that seduced her audiences with her performances, who oozed sex appeal just standing in a bookshop in normal attire, and now that she knew that Danika and Dani were the same person, there was no way that things could ever attempt any kind of relationship.

It would never work between them. Danika could have any woman she wanted; why the hell would she want boring Cliona?

Oli and Niamh make it work.

But Cliona wasn't Niamh...and Danika wasn't Oli.

A gentle but firm knock sounded on the door, and it made her pulse race, her heart pounding against her chest. Cliona knew the knocks of all of her friends and the staff that worked at Rebel Books, and this was not one she recognised. She couldn't face Danika...it was too damn painful.

The knock came again, this time a little louder, followed by that voice that had given Cliona goosebumps when they spoke on the phone. "I know you probably don't want to talk to me, but Niamh and the blonde are giving me the evil eye so you either invite me in, or I'm gonna need to find somewhere else to sleep tonight."

Cliona snorted, rolling her eyes, "The door's open."

Danika slipped inside, closing the door behind her, and then leaned against it. For a moment, neither of them said anything as Cliona leaned back in her chair, rubbing her sweaty palms on the thighs of her jeans. Her mouth was suddenly so dry that Cliona would have given anything for a drink.

"Listen, I'm sorry for rocking up here and being such a bitch. Oli would tell you it's my default mode most of the time."

"You were never like that with me." Cliona heard herself say quietly, and that made Danika give her a half smile.

"Because you were this beautiful woman I was trying to get in my bed. And I could be myself with you."

Cliona felt her face heat, and she ducked her gaze away from Danika's.

"Did you know who I was before we started talking? Did you know I worked with Niamh?" Cliona asked, not really sure that she wanted the answer to those questions, and was relieved when Danika shook her head.

"No. I had no clue. I had forgotten how small Cork was. I only made the discovery when I nosed at Rebel Books socials and saw you and Niamh together doing promo like two days ago."

Cliona blinked in surprise at the realization that as

soon as Danika had found out who she was, she had jumped on a plane and now, she was here, standing in front of her. And while the Dani she'd been chatting to had always lived in London for work, and Cliona might have been inclined to make a go of the long-distance thing, *Danika* would not only go back to London, but would be touring the world for months at a time and Cliona would be here.

Danika let loose a laugh, the sound pebbling Cliona's skin at the sound of it. Cliona had always loved the sound of her laugh, it sounded like sin and sex, and it hadn't been hard for Cliona to imagine them in bed, naked, her body languid and satisfied to the sound of Danika's throaty laughter. Cliona pressed her thighs together and fought the blush that no doubt cast a pink tinge along her cheeks.

"I know. It makes me sound like a fucking stalker seeing you in a picture and getting on a plane to come see you."

Cliona found herself returning Danika's smile, "You should have just said that you came to visit Oli and that seeing me was a bonus."

"Oh, it's definitely a bonus."

There was no mistaking the flirty comment, the sexual undertone to it and it snapped Cliona back to the real world. What was the point in flirting with Danika when nothing could come of it?

Danika must have sensed the change in Cliona's demeanour because she sauntered forward, placed her palms on the desk, and grinned. "So, when can I take you out to apologise properly?"

"You don't have to do that. It's okay. We can be friends." Cliona tried to keep her voice even, even as her heart drummed in her chest.

"I know. But I want to. It's about damn time we had a date, right?"

Cliona wanted to say yes, she really did. It would be so easy to take Danika up on her offer and go out for dinner, to fall back into the easy conversation and banter, and then take Danika back to her place and fall into bed.

"So, what do you say? You and me go grab some food and you can reacquaint me with your city."

It would be a safer bet to sever the tie now. The pain and embarrassment that Cliona had felt after the whole 'catfish' incident was still so raw, and while Danika had been telling the truth, they were just too different, their lives polar opposites. In the end, they would never be the happy ever after that Cliona wanted. Someone who she could come home to and carve a life for themselves.

As much as she wanted Danika, she wanted to protect her heart more.

With a brisk shake of her head, Cliona got to her feet. "Listen, I appreciate the offer but there is no point in going down that road. You and me, we are too different. It would never work. It could only end in one or both of us getting hurt. I think what happened a month ago proved that."

Danika straightened, folding her arms across her chest, and pushing up her breasts and Cliona couldn't stop herself from dropping her gaze to the cleavage and then snapping her gaze back up to a smug expression.

"You sure about that?" Her tone was flippant and held the hint of a challenge in it. However, Cliona had to hold her nerve, and cling to her resolve.

"I'm sure. Our lives are too different, Danika. I go home at night and curl up on the couch to binge a show or read a book. You get up at night to headline stadiums all over the world. I'd like to think that you and me could work based on what? Online interactions? But that wasn't real."

The words tasted like lies to Cliona, and they must have sounded like lies to Danika because she jerked back. "It was fucking real to me until you called a halt to it."

"I thought you were lying to me!" Cliona yelled, surprised at how loud her voice had gotten. She needed to get back control of the situation. To get a handle on Danika, though Cliona knew without a doubt that there was no handling Danika Keane.

"And now you know I'm fucking not," growled Danika as she scowled. "So you can keep telling me and yourself that you don't want to go out with me because we won't work now that you know who I am, but Oli and Niamh have made it work, Jameson and

Sinéad make it work. Hell, even mild-mannered Cathal makes it work with Luna."

"I think you're scared, Cliona," Danika continued, and Cliona shrank back against the wall. "I think you had conveniently tied up your feelings when you thought I wasn't real. Now, I'm real and I'm here and it fucking terrifies you. How 'bout you stop acting like a chicken shit and take a fucking chance?"

Anger flooded her veins as Cliona walked to the door, yanked it open, and then stepped back. "Get the hell out of my office." Danika looked like she wanted to argue but whatever she saw in Cliona's expression made Danika do what she was asked.

The moment Danika had stepped outside, the rockstar turned back to look at Cliona, her eyes defiant and it just angered Cliona even more.

"Oli was right, ya know. Your default mode is bitch." Then Cliona slammed the door so hard it rattled.

CHAPTER SEVEN

Cliona

CLIONA SPENT the rest of the day fuming, her bad mood continuing into the next day's work. After a restless night where Cliona had barely slept, the next day started badly with a box of deliveries left outside in the rain even though all their suppliers knew they were open twenty-four-seven. Cliona had spent an hour on the phone trying to get a replacement order for the damaged books, the confrontation on the phone pulling at the threads of her temper.

Then she had to deal with a bigoted customer. Cliona had heard the woman shouting from her office, had dashed out to see the woman in her sixties having a go at the part-time morning college student, his face pale as the customer pointed a finger at him telling him that they shouldn't display the LGBTQ books so prominently for everyone to have to look at.

There were a few vile and disgusting things said as Cliona walked up to her and told her that if she didn't like the books on sale at Rebel Books, then she could find another bookshop as Cliona was sure that they would have nothing here that suited her tastes.

The woman had looked totally affronted that Cliona would speak to a customer like she had, then she spotted the pride pin on Cliona's denim jacket. The woman hissed, then stormed out. She turned to look back into the shop and Cliona had waved at her, almost laughing when the woman glared at Cliona before vanishing from sight.

After checking to make sure Dillon was okay, Cliona went back into her office to work on the schedule for the next few weeks but found that she couldn't concentrate. She wondered had Danika already gone back to London after yesterday or had she stayed to hang out with Oli and Niamh. Unable to fight the urge, Cliona grabbed her phone and checked social media to get an update. She checked Danika's name against a hashtag, and saw a few pictures of Danika at Cork Airport grinning as she had some selfies taken with fans.

Stealing herself, she went right to Danika's social media accounts, and was not surprised to see that there had been an update a couple of hours ago. Danika had snapped a picture of herself looking all sweaty and her face flushed as she took a picture of the sun rising behind her with the description: *When you can't sleep and go for a run. I'd forgotten how beautiful and quiet Ireland could be. I think I could get used to this!*

What the hell did that mean? Was Danika planning on staying here in Cork?

It wasn't as ridiculous a thought to Cliona when you considered that not only did all of Heartache Melody live and record in Ireland, but now Oli was working on his own home recording studio at his and Niamh's house so he could be at home with Niamh and mini Scott. But Danika wasn't built for the sometimes mundaneness of living in Ireland. I mean, the bars of Cork City didn't live up to the ones in Soho.

Cliona had considered moving to London before she had come out to her parents. It always seemed so inclusive and welcoming, but she had been terrified. She knew it was stupid to hold onto the hope that her parents might one day accept who she is, however, they were her parents, and try as she might, Cliona could never let that go.

Sitting back in her chair, Cliona couldn't help but think of the time she had found the courage to come out to her parents. It wasn't long after she had had her first kiss with a girl, and that had cemented to Cliona that what she had thought all her life was true, that the way most girls felt about boys, Cliona felt about girls.

It had been over the Christmas holidays when Cliona had lied and said she was going to the cinema with friends from school, when she had gone to a house party instead and during a game of spin the bottle, and she had felt her body ignite like it never had for any boy.

The next day, Cliona had texted her brothers to tell them, and they had warned her not to tell her parents when they were not there, but Cliona had wanted to unburden herself, to get it off her chest. Sitting down to dinner, Cliona had pushed her food around the plate and when her mother had asked her what was wrong, Cliona had set her fork down, and pressed her hands into her thighs.

"There is something I need to tell you," Cliona started, her parents halting mid-bite and her mother dropped her fork on the plate.

"Mother of God, you're not pregnant, are you?"

Somehow, Cliona thought that would be the more acceptable sin than the one she was about to admit to, but it did make Cliona laugh a little considering that she would never have that problem.

"I'm not pregnant, mam." Cliona confirmed, the relief on her mother's face was clear for all to see.

This was it. She could either shove it all back down and keep her secret a little longer, or she could be true to herself even if it meant that her parents might reject her. Cliona had been raised to believe that God loved all of his children; so why was it so hard to believe that included the LGBTIQA+ community?

"Get on with it then," my father said gruffly, "The dinner's getting cold."

Digging her nails into her thighs, Cliona blew out a breadth and swallowed hard before she looked up at her parents and sai,. "I'm gay."

There was nothing but silence for a moment, then her father snorted and rolled his eyes. "No you are not. This is the things those teachers are teaching you. Makes you think you are something you ain't."

"It's true, dad. I like girls. I've kissed a girl and it was wonderful and it felt right. I've always liked girls and I always will."

Her mother blessed herself and started to pray as her father set down his fork and knife. "You are not one of those lesbian types. God would not have given us a sinful child. This will not happen under my roof, Cliona. I will contact the priest in the morning, and we will pray the devil out of you."

Tears began to slip free of Cliona's eyes. "I don't need a priest, dad. I need my parents to accept me for who I am. I am gay. I like girls. But I'm still me."

Her father got up so fast from his chair that it scraped along the wooden floor. "If you continue to think like you are, then you are not my daughter. I will not have someone like you under my roof. So you can choose now to reject the path of sin and the devil, or you can walk out of the house tonight. The choice is yours, Cliona."

The choice had never been hers. Cliona was who

she was, and it had taken her a long time to accept that, because of her parents. It was why she sometimes volunteered at an LGBTIQA+ centre and why Rebel Books had a flyer on the notice board for any teens who needed to talk to someone without judgement. They had enlisted Jameson's fiancé Sinéad to help out too since she had qualifications and that.

And while Cliona had dated, she'd never felt like any of her girlfriends were the ones she was meant to be with, though Cliona knew that some people didn't get a happy ever after like in the books she read. Cliona had thought she had found that with Dani – with Danika – but she couldn't stop herself from thinking about her parents and the fact that they considered her damned. The more time she spent feeling lonelier each day, Cliona wondered if she really was damned to be alone.

Shaking that thought from her head, Cliona picked up her phone and looked at the smiling picture of Danika. Cliona was living too safe. Maybe it was time to stop trying to find a partner in online worlds and see what she might find if she opened herself to the chance of meeting someone that would hold her hand in public, who would love her for who she was.

Cliona was certain that person was not Danika Keane, no matter how disappointed that made her feel. The novelty of Cork would wear off for Danika and she could go back to her life and Cliona would get on with hers. There paths would only cross if and when she visited Oli and Niamh, and while Cliona would always feel wistful about what could have been, she would always know that the two of them were better off as just friends, more friends of friends...

Right?

CHAPTER EIGHT

Danika

"DANIKA, you need to be back in London."

Danika rolled her eyes as she poured herself a coffee in Oli and Niamh's kitchen, the call on loud-speaker as she leaned against the window and looked out into the grey rainy day. Bruno, the person from the record label that was assigned to 'manage' her kept droning on.

"The label wants to come back to the table and make some negotiations. They don't want you to just dismiss their ideas right away. You need to take time to consider them."

"Bruno, mate, they want me to agree to do a fucking dance song. They want to hire a choreographer so that we can have dance numbers." Danika told him before she took a sip of her coffee. "They also want to bring in someone to write MY songs for my next album. Fuck that shit."

"They are all just ideas at the moment, Danika. No one is trying to take away your creative control. The label is just eager to lock you back into a contract. You know how it is."

Of course, Danika did. Oli was currently out of contract and the label was trying to lure him back to signing another decade-long contract. Both Oli and Danika made them a lot of money. Danika herself had endorsements from a lot of gothic clothing labels and even sneakers. It was worth millions to her and the record label. And then they wanted her to do a fucking dance song to get played on the radio more and be the "Song of Ibiza Summer."

She'd leave that to Calvin Harris and Joel Corry.

"We also need to speak about Lola." Bruno broached and Danika groaned, letting her head hit the glass of the door.

"Tell ya what, Bruno, let's not. I sacked her. Shit got too weird, and she wasn't acting professional. It was unreasonable for the label to expect me to keep working with her after all the shit she pulled."

Bruno clicked his tongue. "Then you shouldn't have slept with your manager when you were drunk, Danika."

"And she shouldn't have broken into my apartment and gotten into my bed naked like some stalker, Bruno. If I was a man, you'd be out there sprouting about male objectification. You'd be turning the story into a positive spin and all I get is bad girl Danika, you should have realized the woman the label assigned as your manager was infatuated with you."

Lola had been more than infatuated. She had photos in her home of Danika and her together, cut out of magazines. The label also hadn't told her that this was the second time this had happened with Lola, and that first time had been with a movie star.

Lola was a more intense version of Nicollette who used to work for Rebel PR. Danika hadn't noticed her jealously until it was too late, and she'd made the terrible mistake of having sex with her. Lola had taken that as confirmation that Danika and her were an item, and she had become possessive, going so far as to plant a fucking camera in Danika's bedroom.

Danika had wanted to press charges for invasion of privacy, not to mention the sickening knowledge that Lola had watched videos of Danika with other women. The label had persuaded her that it would only cause bad publicity for Danika, that her extensive list of lovers would convince them that Danika had played Lola.

And that was one of the main reasons why she was trying to break away from the record label, why she was so desperate to have a conversation with Oli about the future.

"Danika, are you even listening to me?"

Niamh came into the kitchen then, dressed in a

fluffy robe as she waved at Danika, then frowned at the phone. Danika let Bruno stew for a few minutes and when he repeated himself, Danika pushed away from the patio door and strode over to poor herself more coffee.

"I can hear ya loud and clear, Bruno. But you keep on talking about the same shit and it's wrecking me fucking head. How bout you tell the label I'm taking some much-needed annual leave and put me on out of office for a while?"

Danika could hear Bruno's sigh of frustration down the phone. "And how long should we expect you to be out of office, Danika?"

Flashing Niamh a grin as she pulled out a chair so the pregnant woman could sit down, Danika walked back over to where the phone sat on the counter. "I'll get back to you on that, Bruno. Could be a month, could be six. I haven't decided just yet."

"Jesus Christ, Danika. You can't take six months off. We have offers coming in left and right, we have festival headline offers waiting to be signed off on. You cannot take six months off and do absolutely nothing."

"I won't be doing nothing, Bruno." Danika told the label executive. "I'm gonna write some songs. I'm gonna get a tattoo. I'm going to hang around and see if I have a niece or a nephew. Who the hell knows what else I'm gonna do? Maybe I'll buy a farm and get myself a Netflix series about the Goth and the farm. Actually, that's not a bad name for it."

"Danika!"

Danika could almost see the steam coming out of Bruno's ears as she told him to not bother calling her, that she would reach out when she decided on the farm. She hung up to the sound of Bruno calling her name, then sat down on the seat next across from Niamh.

"Hey, I didn't wake you did I? I sometimes forget to use my indoor voice."

Niamh chuckled, shaking her head. "No, sleep isn't coming to me so well. I got up so as not to disturb Oli. He usually wakes as soon as I do, and I thought he could do with a few hours more."

Danika asked Niamh if she wanted anything for breakfast, laughing when Niamh said she had a craving for rashers and ice cream again. Making herself useful, Danika fried up some rashers and removed a tub of strawberry ice cream from the fridge. Then joined Niamh in eating some rashers and ice cream, and that made the expectant mother laugh.

"I had to see if it tasted as bad as it sounded. But honestly, I've eaten worse."

"Hey, if you were serious about the farm, then you should talk to Sorcha." Niamh said as she ate a mouthful of the weird and wonderful concoction.

"Sorcha?" Danika asked after swallowing her own bite.

"You met her yesterday at the bookshop. Blonde and stunning."

Danika snorted through her nose. "I would not have expected blondie to be a farm girl. That's a pleasant surprise but I do think after yesterday she'd rather bury me under a pile of slurry than tell me about owning a farm. And could you imagine me owning a farm? I'm too much of a city slicker. All that quiet would wreck me head."

Niamh smiled, set down her cutlery, then leaned back in her seat. "Maybe. And Sorcha was only being protective of Cliona. She might look like a Hollywood starlet, but Sorcha is fierce and smarter than her looks give her credit for. If you ever need help with your finances, Sorcha is your girl."

Danika appreciated that Niamh was still talking to her after what had gone down with Cliona, and the way Cliona had called her a bitch in a cold tone had played over and over in Danika's mind since yesterday. It had sat like lead in her stomach.

"Did you mean what you said about staying in Ireland for six months?"

Lifting her gaze to Niamh's, Danika twirled her finger in the end of her ponytail. "Worried I'm gonna want to stay here?"

Niamh's cheeks went a bright pink. "Oh god, no, I didn't mean it like that. I mean you are Oli's sister; you can stay as long as you want. We love having you here."

"That's fucking debateable." Sounded a gruff and sleepy voice as Danika laughed and Oli walked in, shirtless in just a pair of shorts, and it reminded Danika of when they'd shared a dorm. Oli bent and kissed Niamh on the top of her head, then went straight to the coffee and poured himself a mug.

"I'll find my own place if I do decide to hang out for a bit. Last thing you guys need is me hanging out when you have a new arrival incoming."

Had Danika not been looking at Oli, she might have missed the flicker of emotion in his eyes, but thankfully Niamh seemed to miss it. Danika cleared her throat, then got to her feet.

"I need a favour." She said to Oli and he arched a brow. Danika knew that Oli's curiosity would get the better of him.

"Spit it out, Dani. We ain't getting any younger."

"Can you get me in to see that boss ass bitch of yours?"

CHAPTER NINE

Danika

OLI FROWNED AT HER. "Why do you want to see Andi?"

Danika grinned at Niamh. "Don't you love that he knew I was talking about Andi Collins right away?"

"Danika."

Oli's tone made her roll her eyes as she walked over to stand at the opposite side of the kitchen island. "Well, you have the dad tone down already. I want to see Andi because I want Rebel PR to manage me. And I want you and me to set up our own record label so we can do our own stuff like we always wanted to."

With his lips turned downward in a frown, Oli kept his eyes on her. "I can take you to Andi, no hassle. But the other thing is not something I can even think about right now. The record label knows that I have no intentions of signing with them again after how they treated me after the throat thing."

"So that's why they have a hard on trying to get me to resign." Danika ground out, rubbing her temples.

"Negotiations going that bad?" Oli asked as Danika leaned her forehead on the counter and banged it once.

"They want her to do a feature on a dance track." Niamh said softly.

Danika lifted her head to see Oli trying to hold back a laugh. "Who?"

"Calvin." Danika said with a huff.

"Could be worse. Instant hit with Calvin."

"Fuck you." Danika snarled at Oli. "If you like him so much, you do the fucking song with him. I'd rather not alienate my fans by jumping to the mainstream just for royalties."

Oli pulled his phone out of his pocket and dialled a number. "Hey, you still at the Rebel PR offices today?"

Danika couldn't hear the other side of the call but then Oli laughed. "No, it's a business thing. I have a client that's interested in hiring Rebel PR."

Nothing was said for a few seconds and then Oli barked out a laugh and hung up.

"Well?"

Oli grinned, running a hand through his hair. "She said, if you are telling me that Danika is ready to sign up with us then get your ass over here right now and sign the goddamn papers before she changes her mind.

Then she shouted at someone to start dictating a contract."

See this is why Danika wanted to be Andi's client; girl got shit done, and looked good doing it.

Oli told Danika to let him go shower and get dressed, and Niamh rose to do the same, telling Oli that Jameson was coming over to take her to their parents for lunch so to take her time with Danika and Andi. Danika herself went up to her room and changed into jeans and a band tee, then threw on a shirt before she headed down and then Oli was ready.

Jameson Kent, guitarist with Heartache Melody was pulling in as they were about to leave, and after promising to stay long enough to have a drink or two with the band, Oli and Danika drove the short distance from Oli's new gaff to the industrial estate that was quickly becoming its own celebrity village.

Declan's studio and home was sat next to the gym he owned with F1 driver Noah Donovan, and then the Rebel PR building that was still being put together. Hell, even Andi's brother Rhys lived in the apartment above the gym.

When Oli parked the car, he didn't get out, just took off his seatbelt and looked at Danika. "Niamh was worried that you thought we didn't want you to stay with us with what she said. I've been ordered to make sure you know that you can stay as long as you want."

Danika rolled her eyes. "I bloody know that but if I do decide to hang around, I'll get my own place. You two need your own space, especially when mini Scott arrives."

A muscle in Oli's jaw ticked and Danika had to know what the fuck was going on with him.

"Alright spill, Oli. Every time someone mentions the baby or mini Scott, you flinch. Niamh hasn't noticed but I have. Get it off your chest."

Oli's grip on the steering wheel tightened. "Let it go, Dani. It'll be grand."

"Oliver Scott, do not make me call JJ and have him talk to you in that tone of his where it seems like he is disapproving of your life choices."

Like Danika had done to the kitchen table, Oli banged his head against the steering wheel. "It's stupid."

"Probably. But tell me anyways."

Reaching over, Oli pressed a button on the dash and a compartment opened to reveal a small velvet box that Danika knew had to contain an engagement ring. "OLI!!!"

He slammed the compartment shut and lifted his head off the steering wheel. "Stop. I'm not gonna propose."

"Why the fuck not?" Danika demanded.

"I'm fucking terrified she'll say no. Or worse, think that I'm only asking her to marry me because she's having our baby. It's stupid that every time she calls the baby mini Scott, I get annoyed that we won't all have the same last name. Like we won't be a proper family."

Danika reached over and smacked Oli hard on the side of the head. He yelped and rubbed the spot that Danika had walloped and glared at her.

"You can glare at me all you want, but you are an idiot. Niamh loves you and would marry you in the morning if you asked her. It's sickening how in love you two are. But if you are asking her to marry you because you have this hang up about ye all having the same last name, then don't ask her. You and Arthur have the same last name and you guys most certainly aren't a family. Me, you, and JJ don't have the same last name or even share blood, but we are family."

Oli exhaled, then scratched at his chin. "I really do hate when you are the voice of reason. It's unsettling."

Danika laughed, the sound filling the car. "I love you too. Now, about the record label?"

Rolling his eyes as he got out of the car, Oli waited until Danika was out before he said. "One thing at a time. See if you want to stay or if you want to sign with Rebel PR. I haven't decided what I'm gonna do myself yet. I mean, we could do it...right?"

Danika didn't say anything else, knew Oli well enough that she needed to let the idea sit with him for a while as he mulled over all the specifics and formulated a plan. It was how Oli's mind worked. He needed to work out all the finer details before he committed to anything. He might appear spontaneous and carefree, but not many people knew just how much thought Oli actually put into things.

"Thanks for getting me in with, Andi. You think you could see if Cathal had any free time to ink me while I'm here?"

Oli slid his gaze to her as she grinned, a serious look on her face. "Not a chance in hell. I might share Andi with you, but not Cathal, especially when you have a hell of a lot more skin left than I do. That's a deal breaker. Issaac or Darren can sort ya out."

Danika was almost crying with laughter as they strode into the warehouse at what was to be Rebel PR's Irish office. She spotted Andrea Collins coming toward her. The other woman was striking and a badass who had cultivated a successful business with her best friend, and current Rebel Racers CEO, Charlie Coyle.

Andi was grinning as she shoved a pile of papers at Danika, ordering her to sign them.

"Do I at least get to read through it? Have a conversation?" Danika asked even though she had already made up her mind.

"You'll sign, or else why the hell did you want to meet me so urgently? I know what happened with Lola. That woman shouldn't have even been allowed to work with clients. If Rebel PR manages you, you won't have to worry about any of that shit, even if I am engaged to one of my clients and my brother is also a client."

Danika tilted her head, and folded her arms across her chest but didn't say anything so Andi continued.

"This is a family. Once you're in, you're in. We look after our family. It isn't about the money for us, though that helps. We genuinely want the best for you. You don't like a suggestion we make, then we work until we find something you like. But I won't bullshit, or molly coddle you. We're damn good at our jobs, but we aren't your babysitters. I just ask that if you are about to do something that might end up in the media, you give us a heads up first."

"I want you to manage me to start."

"Deal."

Danika had a quick look through the contract, and didn't see anything that threw up any red flags, so she took the pen Andi held out to her, motioned for Oli to turn around, and used his back to sign the contract.

Chapter Ten

Cliona

CLIONA WAS SURPRISED to open her front door and see Niamh standing on the other side, holding up a bag of food and wearing a bright smile. She raised a hand to say goodbye to Oli, who honked the horn and drove off, leaving Cliona to step aside and let Niamh in.

Watching in amusement as Niamh rooted around in Cliona's kitchen, taking out plates and glasses, Niamh turned suddenly, and her mouth formed an "O", "I'm doing it again."

"What?" Cliona asked, taking the food out of the bag.

"Nesting," Niamh said as she pulled out a chair and sat down at the table. "Oli says I've been cleaning and tidying far more than usual but I told him that was silly. Now, I've just come into your house and made myself at home."

Cliona laughed and opened a bag of Taytos. "You do you, Niamh. I'm just happy to see you and that you brought food. Saves me from ordering from Chinese again. I swear I call so much they probably just put the order through when they see my phone number on the screen."

Niamh laughed and went about pushing food in Cliona's direction. They talked about the bookshop, the book they were both currently reading, and other gossip like Nessa's moving-in date, and how Oli was working to get security updated on the apartment.

"I asked Oli how he knew Nessa needed the extra security and he said that something she had said to him one day stuck in his head and he just knew she had seen the darkest side of mankind. He never pressed me to know more or Nessa, but that's one of the many reasons I love him."

The affection in Niamh's tone was evident, and Cliona was thrilled for her friend. Niamh ate some more of her sandwich, then some Taytos and she washed it down with some tea before she said. "Did you hear that Brian and Nicollette broke up?"

Cliona set down her own mug of tea. "No? Who ended it?"

"Nicollette apparently. Andi told me that Nicollette and Brian had been attending some work do and there was an American senator there. A week later, Nicollette handed back her engagement ring and is now in the U.S. about to marry a man twenty years her senior."

Cliona leaned her chin in her hands. "Serves the bastard right. I hope it kills him to know that you traded up and Nicolette would rather go to bed with someone old enough to be her dad."

"He texted me last week."

That was news to Cliona, and she wondered if Oli knew that Brian had been in touch. The fucker had stripped Niamh of her confidence and that lack of belief in herself had almost disastrous consequences for her and Oli. There was no way that Oli knew about this or else he'd be fuming.

"You didn't tell Oli."

Niamh swallowed hard. "No, I didn't. I'm not really sure why but I didn't."

Cliona allowed Niamh a minute to gather her thoughts as she finished her sandwich and ate the rest of her Taytos. Niamh had been staring into her tea, then she lifted her gaze to Cliona.

"He asked me to meet him for dinner. He said he wanted to apologize for how he treated me and that it had taken losing me to realize how much that he loved me."

Hold on a minute, Niamh wasn't falling for that BS, was she?

Her friend let loose a laugh. "Jameson had the exact same expression when I blurted it out to him.

No, I don't love him. I love Oli. It just dragged up some stuff and if I tell Oli, he'll want to stand up for me and I can do that for myself now. I love my life."

That was a relief to hear, and it must have shown on her face because Niamh laughed. "Jameson had that expression too. And I will tell Oli, I just need to find the right time."

That made Cliona pay even more attention, so although all she really wanted to do is find out if Danika was still in Cork, she asked Niamh a different question. "Did you message Brian back?"

Niamh gave a slight bop of her head. "I did it with Jameson. He and Sinéad helped me to reply back and tell Brian that I had no interest in revisiting that part of my life and I was only focused on the family I was creating with Oli. Then he just came back and said he wished me well, but it sounded like he was pissed off I didn't immediately drop everything to go running back to him."

"I mean, even I can see that you traded up. Brian never fit you."

They ate the remainder of their food and then after Niamh went to the bathroom, they went to sit in the living room with more tea. Niamh kicked off her shoes and curled up on the couch and sipped her tea, and Cliona caught her stealing glances at her.

"What? Have I something in my teeth?"

"Why did you never tell me about Danika?"

Oh shit, so they really were gonna talk about Danika now.

"I was embarrassed," Cliona admitted, pulling her knees to her chest. "I really thought that I had been made a fool of, and I didn't want you to know and worry."

"I'm going mad I didn't notice, but with Oli and mini Scott, I've been a terrible friend."

Cliona hated that Niamh would think that. "No. It was all me. Sorcha only knew because it was getting to me. I thought I had found someone like you had, and when I thought it was all fake, I couldn't stop thinking about what a fool I'd been."

"And now?" Niamh broached as she rested her mug on her belly.

"It wasn't fake, but it wasn't real either. She's Danika fucking Keane."

Niamh chuckled, an understanding expression on her face. "I used to think like that with Oli. Every single time I caught him looking at me, I told myself it was nothing. When he flirted with me, I convinced myself it was just who he was and not that he had any interest in me. Hell, even after we had slept together, I just assumed it was another notch on his bedpost. But look at us now."

"Oli and Danika are different people." Cliona countered, but Niamh shook her head.

"Maybe, but they are more similar than you think. Yes, Danika is mouthy and opinionated, but that's just her being Dani. She's kind and considerate. You can see why she and Oli are like siblings, they fit in a way that me and Jamie fit. I think she's more the Dani that you were chatting to, than the fuck you rockstar. Just like Oli is."

That was the one thing that had kept Cliona going back to her feelings for Danika. It was harder to keep up the pretence of who she was when talking to Cliona, than it would be for the time she was on stage. That was the part that Cliona couldn't let go of, because what if it had been real?

"Listen, I wanted to let you know that Danika is staying in Cork for a while."

Cliona rested her chin on her knees. "Okay."

With a warm smile, Niamh went on. "She's trying to figure out some stuff. Career stuff. And I think she misses having Oli so near especially with JJ in the U.S. right now. She had some issues with her previous manager last year and while it's not common knowledge yet, Danika has just signed with Rebel PR."

Cliona wasn't too shocked by what Niamh was saying. It made sense that she would miss Oli, who was her brother in every way that mattered. And Oli had been working with Andi Collins and her firm for years. Danika would trust them because Oli did. But what happened with her old manager?

"So, she'll be staying with you and Oli?"

"For now," Niamh said, a smile curving her lips. "And as much as Oli complains, I know he's happy to have her around. To be fair, she's no trouble. When Oli and me left to come here, she was lying on her stomach in the middle of Oli's current music room, playing a keyboard and scribbling notes on paper. It's just like with Oli only this time, I have to get used to seeing Danika in her underwear."

Cliona had been in the middle of taking a drink and spit it out, as Niamh burst out laughing.

"No? Really?"

Niamh inclined her head. "I'm not lying. The first time it happened, I was all stuttery but Oli came in and didn't even mention it. I forget they used to see each other naked all the time when they roomed together. How the hell is this my life?"

Cliona changed the subject then, and thankfully Niamh took the hint and they chatted away until Niamh's rockstar boyfriend showed up to drive her home to their goddamn mansion.

How the hell was any of this their lives?

CHAPTER ELEVEN

Cliona

CLIONA HAD ENJOYED her lunch with Niamh yesterday, had almost snapped up her offer to come to dinner one night the next week, but asked Niamh if she could think about it. Her friend had hugged her and told her that she was welcome at her home anytime. She said it with a fierceness that Cliona had appreciated, but she didn't know if she was ready for another face-to-face with Danika yet.

Fate, it seemed had other ideas for Cliona. As she left her shift at Rebel Books to head home, stepping out into the surprisingly sunny day, she shielded her eyes from the mid-afternoon glare and almost walked right into Oli and Danika.

Cliona tripped over her feet, and would have ended up on the footpath had Oli not reached out to steady her. When she was steady again, Cliona glanced from Oli to Danika, and just the sight of her was arresting.

Today, Danika looked every bit the goth princess from her music videos. Her black hair was pulled back into a high braid, her eyes looked smoky, and her lips wore an intense black. She was wearing a black sleeveless vest and a pair of black cargos. The only pop of colour she wore was the bloodred sneakers that she wore.

"Hey Cliona, how's things?" Oli asked with a grin.

"Things are good," Cliona said as she dragged her gaze from Danika to Oli. "Where's your better half?"

Oli chuckled, his smile deepening. "Niamh and her mam have gone on a spa day. Niamh is having some weird pregnancy massage thing and her mam went with her. Me and Dani were just over at Rebel Ink trying to get Danika in for a tattoo."

Cliona took the opportunity to glance at Danika, and found the other woman looking at her.

"Would you believe that we spent a good portion of the time arguing that Oli didn't want Cathal to tattoo me? Cathal was highly amused and even the other lads started to try and persuade me that they needed to tattoo me."

Oli ran his hand through his dark hair. "It's bad enough that I have to share Cathal with Luna. You don't get to steal him too."

Danika burst out laughing, elbowing Oli in the stomach. "This idiot was asking Cathal about tattoo removal so he could get more done. He really is that insane."

"It's not my fault that me and Cathal met late in life."

Cliona let loose a chortle of laughter. "Now I know why Niamh calls Cathal your tattoo husband. It's your version of a work wife."

This time, Oli nudged Danika. "See, Cliona gets it."

"That's totally not what she said, but whatever helps you sleep at night."

The conversation was almost normal, like they were all friends and not that there was starting to be a crowd gathered looking at Oli and Danika. Cliona shifted on her feet, as Oli glanced behind him, then focused back on Cliona like he dealt with this every day. He probably did.

"Niamh said she asked you to come to dinner next week," Oli said suddenly, taking Cliona by surprise.

"I...Ugh...Ya, she did."

An awkwardness filled the space between them, as Danika's gaze narrowed, suspicion in her eyes.

"What she means is that she would love to come for dinner, as long as it doesn't involve me."

"I didn't say that," Cliona argued, though there wasn't much fight in her tone because it was sort of true.

"You didn't have to. Just tell Oli what night suits you and I'll make myself scarce. I'm sure I can find some way to amuse myself for a couple of hours. So, don't not come to the house on my account."

Danika stalked away then, leaving her standing there with Oli, who looked amused by the interaction. "You've gotten under her skin, yano?"

Cliona turned around to see Danika's form heading around a corner. "I didn't mean to upset her. I just didn't want to make it awkward by coming to dinner. She is your guest."

"And you are Niamh's family. Danika is mine but I didn't mean about the dinner."

Cliona must have looked puzzled, as Oli leaned against the wall. "Danika pretends that she doesn't care if you like her or not, but she does. And when she likes someone, she thinks all it will take her to get a woman to bed, is the fact that she is Danika Keane, rockstar."

"Oli, you don't have to explain Danika to me..."

"But I do," Oli said, his smile tired. "Danika's the reason why I'm so successful. Danika became my family after my mam tried to kill me and my dad, well, let's just say he's a piece of shit who will never know their grandchild. And I know she likes you. She was telling me all about this girl she met online for months, and I tried to warn it that it probably wouldn't work out, and she said, it would, and do you know why?"

Cliona wasn't sure she wanted to know what Oli had to say, because it might shatter Cliona's resolve to keep her distance from Danika. But a tiny sliver of her just craved to know what Danika really felt.

"Why?" Cliona heard herself say, her heart thundering in her chest.

Oli reached out and gripped Cliona's shoulder. "Dani smiled wider than I have ever seen her smile and told me that her mystery woman knew her for her, that she got her. While everyone wanted Danika Keane, you wanted Dani. And that meant that you might see passed how she was portrayed in the media."

Her heart stuttered in her chest. "Oli, I'm not cut out to date a rockstar."

"Niamh thought that once upon a time. And look at us now...the epitome of domestic bliss."

That eased the tension in Cliona as she laughed. "Niamh is very, very lucky to have found you. It's hard to find someone that gets you and you get them."

"I'm the lucky one. And you could be too, Cliona. Don't look for obstacles when the world already has an idea about who should get to love. I might be biased but beyond the swearing and the crassness, is a heart of gold and maybe, just maybe, Danika is another rockstar who just needs a girl in a bookshop to love her...flaws and all."

With a final squeeze of Cliona's shoulder, and after making Cliona promise to come to dinner, Oli walked away from her, and in a moment of madness, Cliona called Oli's name to make him stop.

"Tell Niamh I'll text her about dinner. And tell Danika I'll unblock her number. If she's hanging around, then we might as well be friends."

Oli grinned, then jogged to catch up with Danika, leaving Cliona to make her way home, after unblocking Danika's number like she said she would. The conversation with Oli had confused Cliona even more as she walked down the street to where she had parked her car. She was so lost in her own thoughts that she almost missed the couple walking toward her.

Five years since Cliona had seen them, her parents looked older than she'd expected. She ground to a halt, would have to get by them to get to her car. There would be no avoiding them if she wanted to get to her car, and if she turned around now and went back to the bookstore, and they saw her, then they would be winning.

Her mother had yet to notice her, but her father had, his stern gaze landed on Cliona as he frowned, and grabbed hold of his wife's arm. It was then her mother stopped talking and looked right at Cliona. The world seemed to stop moving as Cliona sucked in a lungful of air and just stood there, gawking at the two people who had shunned her.

Cliona didn't know what to do, or what to expect, although it shouldn't have surprised her that her father all but dragged her mother to the opposite side of the road before they continued on their journey. Her pulse pounded so loud in her ears that they rang, and her hands trembled like she was a fifteen-year-old again, frightened of what her parents might say when she came out.

And now they crossed the street like she had some disease they might catch.

Cliona made it back to her car, got behind the wheel, and then sat in the car for a really long time, the sun no longer high in the sky, and darkness creeping in. It took forever for her hands to stop shaking until she felt like she could drive herself home. There was just so much she needed to make sense of in her mind, and seeing her parents like that had dragged up so much pain that she almost didn't hear her phone beep.

Glancing down, Cliona saw a gif from Danika like they used to send to one another, and it made her smile for a moment before she lost control of her emotions and allowed herself to cry.

CHAPTER TWELVE

Danika

DANIKA WAS STILL FEELING a little off-kilter a couple days after sending Cliona the little gif. She'd stared at her phone while she saw the message being read, then nothing for about an hour. Her mood had soured, making her retreat to her room in Oli's house so as not to subject them to the dark fucking raincloud that hung over her head.

When a response came in about an hour later, Danika had been so surprised that she had dropped her phone on the floor and scrambled off the bed to check and see if she had smashed it. Not exactly the most rock-star move. Thankfully, the screen was grand, the message from Cliona a cat laughing gif and it made Danika smile.

Dots had appeared on the screen as if Cliona was

typing, then they stopped, and Danika sent back another gif and that was it. She'd heard nothing in the two days that followed. To say Danika was disappointed would be an understatement.

When Oli had told her that Cliona had unblocked her number and that she would come to dinner, Danika had felt a spark of hope ignite inside her chest. Well, that was fucking doused with the new radio silence from Cliona. Danika didn't want to be the one to push too hard, and freak Cliona out with her being so persistent.

She also wasn't a glutton for punishment, and shouldn't waste time trailing after a woman who obviously didn't want her now that she knew who Danika was.

Her phone rang then, dragging her out of her thoughts and Danika glanced down at the screen, rolling her eyes. Bruno's name flashed on her screen, and she silenced it, then put the thing on do not disturb before she turned it over so she didn't have to look at it. Her phone had been hopping today, but not with anything that she actually wanted, and Danika was in no mood for pleasantries.

"You should really answer that."

Danika tilted her head up and looked at Niamh. The other woman was lying down on the couch, her legs up over a pillow, a book resting on just before the curve of her stomach. Her brunette hair had been braided down the sides and she hadn't taken her eyes off her book when she spoke.

Oli had to go to London to deal with a few things, so Danika and Niamh were spending some quality time together. It was Danika who suggested it, because Oli was torn between having to take the early flight out and the late flight back, leaving Niamh alone. Danika said she was only planning on messing about with some songs, so would keep Niamh company all day.

To be fair, Danika and Niamh had barely spent any alone time together. Danika had known that Oli was utterly obsessed with Niamh Kent the moment she'd heard him talk about her, and then, seeing them together, it was obvious to anyone that they were a perfect fit.

"It's only Bruno. I do not have the patience to deal with his nagging today. He's still harping on about that bloody dance track, and I really don't wanna smash my phone because I hurled it at the wall."

Niamh laughed, shaking her head but she didn't say anything. Danika turned back to the keyboard that was on the floor in front of her. She herself was laying on her stomach, notebook next to her with lyrics written for some songs she was working on. She was frustrated that the songs weren't flowing like they usually did, sometimes obsessively, consuming her until hours had passed and she hadn't eaten or drank.

Danika tinkered with the keys for a little bit, struggling to come up with a melody that might work for one of the songs that she was working on. At this rate, if Danika couldn't get an album worth of songs written, she'd never convince Oli to start up their own record label.

Flipping over her phone, Danika got out the drumming app she had and played the little drumbeat she had tapped into it when thinking about the song. Focusing on the tempo, Danika let her fingers glide over the keys, and began to sing a few of the lines of the song.

It wasn't like a lot of her in-your-face songs that had propelled her into stardom. It was a rockier song, yes, edgy in its own way, but Danika was tired of being the poster girl for women who wanted to give a middle finger to the patriarchy. Yes, Danika knew that she had started off like that, but what eighteen-year-old woman who just happened to be a lesbian, didn't want to help start a movement?

Danika had been so engrossed in the song that she hadn't realized that Niamh had sat up and smiled down at Danika. Propping herself up on her elbows, Danika arched a brow, and traced the way Niamh's hand rubbed her belly.

"You okay?"

Niamh's smile deepened. "Yup. I think Mini Scott likes the song. Of course he would though. When Oli plays and sings, mini Scott kicks up a storm. Jameson's been singing to the baby too; said he wants his niece or nephew to know the sound of his voice. Oli thinks it's absolutely hilarious that the moment a heavy rock or metal song comes on the radio, the baby moves like it's in the mosh pit, but when some pop song comes on, absolutely nothing."

Danika barked out a laugh, then got up off the floor and went to sit down beside Niamh, moving the pillow she'd been resting her legs on out of the way. "Well, if the baby gets Oli's musical genes, I hope they get your looks, because Oli before the glow-up was not as cool as he looks now."

"He showed me a picture of him on our first date, though, I didn't think of it as a date," Niamh mused with a softer smile. "It's hard to imagine that he was this nerdy teen. Or that standing beside you and JJ, that Oli was the one who would be overlooked."

Cupping her breasts as Niamh let loose a startled sound, Danika chuckled. "It's the girls. Being a lesbian in a school full of boys didn't mean that they didn't notice that I had tits. One of the few good things I inherited from my mother." Danika let her gaze drop to Niamh's breasts then slowly dragged her eyes back up, a faint blush on Niamh's cheeks. "But I think you know what that's like. Although pregnancy has given you what, a cup size more?"

Niamh put her hands over her face. "I am not talking about my pregnancy boobs with you, Danika. Oh my god, I'm discussing my boobs with Danika Keane. This is insane."

Danika laughed so hard she had tears streaming

down her face. Poor Niamh. She really wasn't prepared for the fact that they were all family now, and she had to get used to having Danika around, saying weird and inappropriate shit.

Swiping at her eyes, Danika shrugged. "Hey, Oli did tell you I don't have a filter. Did he tell you that when he pointed you out to me, I told him that he needed to make a move, or I would totally try and turn you?"

"You did not!" Niamh exclaimed, amusement in her eyes.

Danika grinned. "I might have been the one who egged him on before Jameson's party when I listed out all of your attributes and how all your curves were enticing. I'd never seen him so pissed at me. But sometimes Oli can get too far in that big brain of his and he needs to be shoved off the cliff."

Niamh didn't laugh. No, instead she lunged forward and embraced Danika. "Thank you. I know that he might have persisted on his own, but if you gave him the push to keep putting himself in my proximity, then I am forever grateful."

Danika wasn't sure she was comfortable with the praise Niamh was heaping on her, so she did what she always did in an awkward situation. She responded with an inappropriate comment. "Grateful enough to let me cop a feel?"

Niamh smacked her shoulder and rolled her eyes. "Now I definitely know that you and Oli are related.

He said the same thing before he left this morning when he helped me tie my shoelaces."

Danika grinned and leaned back in the seat, tucking her legs underneath her. "Hey, I'm only a woman, and you are gorgeous. But listen, if that's off the table, then Dani is a great name for a boy or a girl, yano."

"Not you too!" Niamh rolled her eyes, then Niamh worried at her lip. "Will you tell me some stories about Oli? I'm not asking you to tell me any secrets, but you are his sister and I know there must be things I don't know. But I'd like to."

Danika hopped off the couch, and looked over at a puzzled Niamh. "If we are gonna go down the this is your life of Oli Scott, then we need some tea and those fancy biscuits you hide in the sugar tin. Must be the Cork in me but I've slowly become addicted to that Barry's Tea you love. I'll be right back."

Chapter Thirteen

Danika

THE DAY after hanging out with Niamh, Danika found herself at the Heartache Melody studio, where the band was working on some songs for some performances that they were doing next week to promote the release of their debut album. She could tell the band was nervous as hell as they talked about all the things Andi had lined up for them, including a few pop-up gigs in Ireland and the UK.

She'd been there with Oli, who had dropped Niamh off at Rebel Books before they came over to the studio, for about an hour when Andi had come in with a box, the biggest grin on her face. She set the box down on the coffee table in the rehearsal space and opened the box and held up a completed vinyl of the album.

Rhys and Luna whooped and rushed over, while Jameson came over a little slower, but Declan kept retuning his guitar, and Danika could see the look of blind panic in his eyes. Declan Walsh gave off the impression that he was a gruff, no bullshit singer in a rock band, but Danika could tell that he and Oli were very much alike. Oli had once delayed an album because when he listened to the final cut, he hated his vocals on one track and wanted to rerecord it.

Declan looked like he was contemplating throwing the album in the bin.

He must have sensed her eyes on him because Declan looked in her direction, arched a brow, and shrugged. Danika winked and jumped up off her seat to grab one of the vinyls, and a sharpie from the table, then walked over and made Declan sign it. He rolled his eyes, but did what she asked. Danika made the rest of the band sign it, then she went over to the wall where Declan had an impressive array of guitars hanging on the wall.

Pausing as she grabbed a Heartache Melody tee from the boxes of merch, Danika stripped off her tank top to the exasperated sound of people shouting her name as she ignored them, then set her phone on a shelf, then pressed go live on her social media.

"All right, motherfuckers! I'm in Cork today listening to my buddies in Heartache Melody get pumped up for their debut album release next week and you guys ain't gonna want to fucking miss this."

Danika held up her signed vinyl with a grin. "Perks of being friends with the band. Early copy and I made them all sign it. Preorder your copy now and check out the band once they hit the road next week to do some promo. The best band to come out of Ireland since me and Oli Scott!"

The band was laughing when she finished as she grabbed her other tee but decided to keep the Heartache Melody t-shirt. Oli bumped her fist, as Declan told the rest of the band to get back to practicing. Rhys told Declan he needed a minute to call Shay and show her the album, considering Luna was already calling Cathal to show him before she hung up and went back behind her drumkit.

Andi was looking at Declan, who still hadn't moved to check out the albums Andi had brought in, his expression tense, his body stiff. He glanced at the door, as if he was about to stalk outside and drag Rhys back in by the scruff of his neck if he didn't come back in soon.

Danika nudged Oli, then inclined her head to Declan. Oli jumped to his feet and asked Declan if he wanted to do a run through of Never Back Down, the song on the album that Oli featured on. Oli mentioned that he would be in London for their gig, and he'd be happy to surprise fans with a secret collab on the night.

As Declan grumbled that they had to wait for Rhys, Danika was already behind the keyboard, bumping her fist against Luna's as she had strolled up.

Danika was used to being the front woman of her shows, there was only the rare few occasions that she got to show off her skills on the keyboard or piano, and Oli had taught her how to play a guitar, so this was fun for her.

Declan's frown turned into a wicked grin and Danika saw Andi pull out her phone to record it. Jameson started the intro to the song and Danika joined in on the keyboard, and it was electric. Declan and Oli bounced off one another as they sang, and Danika just soaked it all in. It must be wonderful to share this feeling all the time with the people who were your family. This was why she wanted Oli to agree to their record label, so she could share this kind of feeling with her brother every day.

Rhys came back in and stood beside his sister, a silly grin on his face as Declan called him forward, and Rhys went up to the mic and sang the lyrics with Declan and Oli. When the song ended, Declan was laughing as he clapped Oli on the back and nudged Rhys.

"We totally need to record that as a special edition song."

Rhys ran a hand through his hair. "Andi recorded it. No doubt she'll post it as promo. That was fucking ace."

Declan called for the band to take a break, went over to the bar in the corner and asked what everyone was drinking. Rhys came over to where Danika was behind the keyboard. "Trying to take my job?"

Danika grinned at him. "I look so much better than you with my top off. Maybe I'll try that for my next video. No tee just a leather jacket."

Rhys barked out a laugh. "Isn't that what you wore on the MTV awards the first year you performed?"

Danika arched a brow as if to ask how the hell Rhys knew that, when Declan shouted over. "He had that poster on his wall, Danika."

She'd never seen Rhys blush before, but the man who Danika had always thought of as a fuckboy, but who was now in a committed relationship with Shay Gleeson of Rebel Ink, however this painted him in another light altogether.

Rhys turned away before Danika could say anything more, so she filed the information away for another day. They lapsed into an easy conversation about the bands upcoming gigs, and Oli asked about plans for a second album.

Andi, had come over to sit on the edge of Declan's chair, her boyfriend resting a hand on her thigh as he sipped his beer. She told Oli that once all the promo stuff was out of the way, they would take December and January off so Jameson could be around when Niamh had the baby, and they had Noah Donovan and Charlie Coyle's wedding as soon as the season ended.

Danika didn't know much about F1, but Oli had

mentioned the other day that Noah had taken things up a notch this season and after his loss last year, he was already like fifty points ahead. Oli asked both Declan and Andi, and Jameson, who were all planning weddings, when they planned to walk down the aisle.

Declan glanced up at Andi, who shrugged. "I did offer to get married in Vegas and you said our families would kill us."

Jameson saved Declan then by saying him and Sinéad were planning on spring 2025, and that they had looked at venues so should have a definite date soon. Oli glanced down at his shoes then, and Danika noted that everyone was looking at him, including Niamh's brother Jameson.

Jameson shifted his gaze to Danika, who shook her head and mouthed that she was dealing with it. She knew that Jameson and herself would talk about it later, but Danika was grateful when Jameson grinned, changing the subject.

"So, as we are talking about album number two, it just occurred to me that we had Oli on the first, Danika should be on the second one."

Well, wasn't that an absolutely epic idea. Danika perked up as she grinned, reaching out to click her bottle with Jameson.

"I haven't been able to get Dani on one of my albums yet. You can't steal her first."

"To be fair, Oli," Declan began, his face a mask of

indifference, but there was amusement in his eyes. "You did borrow Luna for a live performance first."

Jameson took a drink of his beer, then leaned back in his seat, resting one of his long legs over the other. "Dec's right. We loaned you Luna, you paid us back by appearing on the album. Then you blackmailed Andi to appear on your new album, with Dec as producer. So it seems only fair that Danika gets to feature on album two, and you can help produce it."

Oli opened his mouth then closed it, as if he knew there was no arguing with Jameson's logic. Danika hadn't felt this excited and happy in fucking ages.

Chapter Fourteen

Cliona

When Cliona had finally told Sorcha about her run in with her parents, Sorcha had been adamant that they were gonna go for a few drinks and not think about shitty parents. Cliona knew that Sorcha didn't really have shitty parents, they just wanted Sorcha to settle down with a nice man and take over the running of the family farm.

Sorcha had no interest in running the farm, though she did continue manage all the financial aspects of it. Her parents just didn't understand that Sorcha was wild at heart and running a farm would never be what her friend wanted.

They had finished up their weekly staff meeting and were waiting for Oli to come get Niamh, and

Cliona was disappointed when it was just Oli in the car. Cliona knew she had left Danika hanging after what happened and there was no going back on that now. But she had hoped to see her and explain what had happened and why she'd not texted back in so long.

Oli greeted Niamh with a firm kiss on the lips, wrapping his hand around her waist as they all walked out, saying goodbye to Nessa who was just about to start her night shift. Oli had parked his car right on the road, as he opened the door for Niamh.

"Where are you two ladies off to looking all glam?" Oli asked.

Sorcha laughed, her hands on her hips. "We are going to drink copious amounts of alcohol that we will regret in the morning."

Oli glanced at Cliona, who shrugged. "What Sorcha said."

Taking out his phone, Oli shot off a text and then it chimed straight away. "Heartache Melody are having a lock in at Luna's dad's pub. I'm heading back once I drop Niamh off at her mam's. You ladies are more than welcome to come along. Luna said the more the merrier."

Sorcha was almost buzzing with excitement at the invite, and Oli saw Cliona hesitate before she shrugged and got into the back seat of Oli's car. Cliona glanced out the window as they drove, stopping to drop Niamh at her mams, telling Oli that she wasn't up to dealing with drunk musicians. Oli offered to stay, but Niamh just kissed his cheek.

"No, go have fun and I'll hang here with the parents tonight. Come get me in the morning and we can go for breakfast, although mam will probably cook a big breakfast if I tell her you and Jameson were out drinking. You better tell my brother mam will expect him...Danika too."

Once Oli had walked Niamh to her mams, they drove the short distance to Sullivan's bar, Oli holding the door open for them. Sorcha strode in with that confidence she had and was immediately greeted by the band. Cliona herself knew most of the band from the time they spent in the bookstore, and had even gone out with them a few times. She glanced around the bar, but didn't see Danika as Luna asked her what she wanted to drink, handing her a bottle of cider when she asked for it.

Music was thumping as Jameson disappeared out one of the doors, and was gone for a while as she chatted to the band. She heard Luna shout, then was shocked when Emil Anderson came from upstairs and went to help Luna with the drinks. Emil was a Danish football legend and the boyfriend of Luna's twin brother Luke.

It was then that Luna's boyfriend, Cathal Horgan, the owner of Rebel Ink came in the door carrying bags filled with food. Everyone cheered, the tattoo artist rolling his eyes as Luna leaned over the bar to kiss her boyfriend hard on the lips.

Cliona took a second to look around the bar and it hit her then that most of the famous people in the bar were dating musicians. Jameson and Sinéad, Luna and Cathal, Rhys and Shay, hell even Oli and Niamh. And they all made it work...

Cliona heard a howl of laughter that sent a shiver along her spine as Danika walked out from the back with Jameson as they chatted, then her eyes seemed to land on Cliona and a cautious smile curved her lips. Jameson said something to Danika, and she shoved him, before she rolled her eyes.

Rather than coming straight to Cliona, Danika ducked under the bar and helped Luna and Emil take the food that Cathal had brought and started setting it out on the bar for people to help themselves. Cliona finished her cider in one big gulp, and was surprised when Emil handed her another drink as she set down her glass.

"You look like you need that."

"Thanks. I'm Cliona, I work with Niamh."

Emil smiled at her; his handsome face friendly as he inclined his head. "It's nice to meet you, I'm Emil."

It was on the tip of Cliona's tongue to say she knew who he was but thought it might be weird since she was trying to pretend, she hung out with famous people all the time. Instead, Cliona took a sip of her drink, and then said. "Where's Luke?"

The pure look of love in Emil's eyes spoke volumes of the couple's relationship. "I flew in a days earlier than expected. He is currently in Japan at the Grand Prix week to cheer on Noah and Quinn. I admit I was rather worried since it was the first race he had been too since his accident but so far, he is having a great time."

Luke Sullivan had been an up-and-coming F1 superstar when he was almost killed in a crash in Australia, but thankfully, he had survived, but it had ended his F1 career. The last Cliona had heard was that Luke was gonna be racing a rally car in the not-so-distant future.

Luna called Emil then and he offered Cliona a smile before he went over to Luna. Danika was watching her, and Cliona had to drag her gaze away as the band got to their feet when Luna told them all to grab a plate and head into the other room.

Cliona put a few bits on a plate as she walked in with Sorcha and took a seat, looking at the stage, and the set-up, wondering if the band was gonna do a performance. Hell, was Danika?

Niamh had told her that the band and the musicians liked to wind down by doing little, what they called, karaoke sessions, and it looked like they were gonna have one tonight. Sinéad and Shay arrived while she was walking into the other room, as Rhys and Jameson came in with their partners.

Everyone was in good spirits as they ate and drank,

with Emil and Luna going back and forth to make sure that everyone had a full glass. Cliona picked at her food, and was surprised when Luna's boyfriend Cathal sat down beside her. Since both Rebel Books and Rebek Ink had been opened around the same time, she had known Cathal for years and had even gotten tattooed by him once before.

"They can be a bit much when they all get together, right?" Cathal said after taking a drink from his beer. "Wait until you get the Rebel Racers lads in the mix and shit can get pretty surreal."

Cliona laughed, shifting in her seat as she replied. "You went on tour with them... I'm surprised some TV producer hasn't approached you to do a TV show."

Cathal pressed his lips together looking sheepish and Cliona gasped. "Oh my God!!"

"Don't tell Luna. She'll want me to do it. I was not built to be on TV."

Cliona looked over to where Luna Sullivan was standing. It hadn't occurred to Cliona just how much Luna and Danika were alike. Not in appearance, but in attitude. They both had this no fucks given attitude and bucked at conforming. They were unapologetic with how they lived their lives and Cliona was envious of that...she wished she had the nerve to be that way.

Luna bounced as she went up behind the mic and everyone cheered. "All right, party people, who wants to go first?" When no one moved, Luna scowled.

"Come on, someone volunteer or I am totally singing myself and no one wants that."

Cathal groaned beside her, so either Luna had a terrible singing voice, or she would do a song that would embarrass her boyfriend. Cliona glanced around to see if anyone was gonna volunteer, as she saw Rhys get to his feet, strip off his tee as everyone hooted, and then he threw back on his leather jacket much like Cliona had seen him do on stage before.

Danika smacked her leg in laughter as Rhys went on the stage with Jameson on guitar and did an acoustic version of Danika's song, *"Just a Bitch"*. Rhys flipped them all off as he did a great job of performing the hit, and when he finished, Danika was up on the stage grabbing his face in her hands and planting a kiss on the shocked rocker's lips.

When Shay shouted a fake annoyed hey, Danika leapt off the stage and did the same to Shay, and it made Cliona wonder what it would be like to be kissed senseless by Danika Keane.

Goddammit, she needed another drink.

Chapter Fifteen

Cliona

Cliona was up and out of her seat before anyone could stop her. Cathal had said her name softly, but Cliona was already at the bar. But of course, the one time she desperately needed a drink, there was no one in the bar serving. It felt rude to just duck behind the bar and grab a drink herself, so Cliona just rested her elbows on the bar as she heard Declan's voice ring out and waited for someone to come and grab her a drink.

"Rhys singing wasn't that bad."

Cliona spun round and swallowed hard to see Danika standing in front of her. There was no way to blunt the impact of having her so close, and no way to stop Cliona from running her eyes over Danika's curvy frame. Her black silky hair was back off her face, with just the barest hint of makeup on her eyes and face, but her lips were painted a dark purple.

Her full breasts stretched the Heartache Melody tee that she wore, the hem cinched up and tucked up to reveal a toned stomach with pale creamy skin, her outfit completed by a pair of loose army-coloured cargos that emphasised her hips and Cliona knew that if Danika turned round, would showcase her spectacular ass. The barest hint of black lace peeked out from the waistband of the cargos, and Cliona's heart raced at the images that flashed in her mind.

Danika sighed when Cliona didn't say anything, just walked around the bar, and dammit, her ass did look fucking damn good in those pants. The rockstar ducked behind the bar and pulled a pint of cider for Cliona, sliding it over to her.

"Thanks."

"No problem," Danika said in reply, but her tone was kinda clipped, like she was trying hard not to say anything else that might upset Cliona.

Then Danika opened her mouth as if to say something, but Luna came bounding out. Her gaze darted from Cliona to Danika, then back again with a grin. "Am I interrupting something?"

"No." They both said together, then glared at each other as Luna barked out a laugh.

"Riiiiight. Dani, you wanna make Rhys's head explode and sing a song with him?"

Danika grinned, coming out from behind the bar

and asking Luna what song had she in mind, and when Luna told her, Danika grinned like a madwoman. "That's bloody genius. Come on. Call me a fucking genie because I'm making all his wishes come through."

Danika strode into the other room as Luna looked at Cliona. "Rhys had a crush on Danika and Danika found out. We are all encouraging her to take the piss out of him, which makes us terrible people."

Cliona felt herself smile despite herself. "He's not expecting Danika to drag him onstage?"

"Hell no! Come on, we don't want to miss his face."

They made it into the other room just in time to see Danika drag Rhys on stage, and then call Luna on stage. The drummer got behind her kit, as Rhys looked like he would rather be anywhere but on the stage right now.

"So, a little birdy has told me that this is Rhys's getting ready to go out song, and we are gonna do our best to sing it for ya, aren't we, Rhys?"

The rockstar glared at his friends in the band, who all started to whoop then Danika held up her hand and said into the mic. "Am I throwing you off?"

Rhys said nothing, just frowned, staring at Danika as she rolled her eyes and said it again, this time Rhys responded, and Danika grinned and Cliona couldn't help but laugh as Luna started to drum and the two singers started to sing Nelly Furtado's *Promiscuous Girl*, Rhys singing the Timbaland side of it.

Cliona was mesmerized by the sway of Danika's hips as she moved to the music, how good Danika and Rhys sounded, though Cliona knew that Danika would sound good reading a phonebook. Rhys started to loosen up, and fully immerse himself in the experience, moving himself as he sang with a grin on his face.

The song ended too soon as everyone got to their feet and clapped and cheered, with Rhys' girlfriend Shay yelling the loudest. Rhys flipped them off, but he was grinning as he held out his fist to Danika, and she returned it.

Oli came and sat down beside Cliona as Declan and Jameson went to the stage. He nudged Cliona's knee. "You aren't having fun, are you?"

"I am," She protested, then sighed when Oli looked at her with an I smell bullshit expression. "She's a presence, isn't she?"

"Always has been," Oli confirmed, running a hand through his hair. "She once walked into our school assembly in nothing but a pair of boxers and bra when she was pulled up for being a temptation to the boys in the school. The first time she hadn't been wearing anything other than the school uniform, so she wanted to prove a point. She got suspended for it, the stunt, and on the first day back after her suspension, she did it all over again, this time, with me and JJ by her side."

Cliona wasn't shocked by what Oli said...she knew

it must have been hard for Danika in a school full of boys, especially when she had no interest in any of their advances. She glanced at Danika, who was chatting to Rhys and Shay by the stage as Jameson and Declan finished their song. There was a lull then as everyone chatted, and everyone nearly missed Danika getting on the stage as she hooked her phone up to the speakers and music started to play as Danika spelled her name into the mic and then launched into Ciara's *Like a Boy*.

"*So, who's on your list of celebs you'd wanna get naked with?*" *Cliona said down the phone.*

"*Ciara,*" *Dani replied without a second thought.* "*That Like a Boy video almost made me orgasm just watching it.*"

Danika had told her that she was a fan of the singer, even though it wasn't her usual taste when they had been on the phone a couple of months ago. It was only when the music breakdown came on and Danika did the dance routine, and everyone just looked at her in shock, did Cliona realized just how much that video and the song had inspired Danika.

Cliona looked at Oli, who was the only one who didn't seem surprised, just had a smug smile on his face. Danika finished up her song, and the place erupted as she bowed, and then called Luna up. She said something to the drummer and Luna's eyes went wide before Danika went to the mic. "Oli, get your ass up here!"

Cliona had never, ever seen Oli and Danika perform together, and it must have shown in her expression because Oli just shrugged. "We haven't been on stage together since secondary school. This will be fun."

Watching as Oli went on stage, Danika whispered to him and Oli smirked, then reached for Jameson's guitar when the other man gave him the nod. Oli played a few chords, then stepped back to where Luna was on the drums and Danika counted them in.

Luna started, then Oli strummed the base guitar and Cliona was already leaning forward in her seat. Danika started to sing, her eyes focused on Cliona. Somehow, this song was for Cliona reminding her that Danika was who she was, a rockstar, and she wasn't about to apologise for it.

The provocative lyrics of Rihanna's *Rockstar*, coupled with Luna's drumming and Oli's guitar playing, sounded as if the song had been written for Danika. The way Danika's hands touched her body as she sang heated Cliona's entire body.

The room felt suddenly too warm, like someone had cranked up the heat and that person was Danika Keane. Not once during the song had Danika taken her eyes off of Cliona, and now, others were starting to look at her too. She squirmed under the weight of their curious eyes, bringing her eyes back to clash with Danika's.

Danika's lips quirked up at the corners as she kept

on reminding Cliona that she was a rockstar, that this was her world and Cliona was just living in it. However, Cliona was enthralled by Danika, and the presence she had on stage and if Danika walked off that stage right this moment and claimed her lips, then Cliona would have let her. She had never wanted Danika more than she did right now.

The smugness on Danika's face told Cliona that Danika knew exactly where Cliona's thoughts had drifted, and that snapped Cliona from her lustful haze. Her knickers were damp and she had the most intense throbbing between her legs as Danika traced her lips with her tongue and Cliona could almost imagine what it would feel like to have that tongue trying to ease the throbbing.

Cliona was in trouble...very sexy rockstar kinda trouble that she didn't know she wanted to get out of.

Chapter Sixteen

Danika

MAYBE SHE COULD BLAME it all on the alcohol, but up until after she had performed with Oli and Luna, Danika had only drunk two beers. By the time she had a moment after the performance to seek out Cliona, the person solely responsible for her frustration, she had vanished.

Danika had then proceeded to try drowning out that frustration by very impressively drinking an entire bottle of vodka by herself. She'd woken the next day with the mother of all hangovers. She had felt so rough that when Oli had come to ask her if she wanted to come have breakfast at Niamh's parents' house with them, and Jameson and Sinéad, Danika had groaned and hidden under the duvet.

The tense interaction in the bar had pulled on Danika's insecurities, and she wanted Cliona to know that Danika was tired of being the villain in Cliona's story. Danika had worked too hard to be who she was, to be happy with who she was, but these past few months, Danika felt like she had forgotten all that she had done, and how she had fought to be where she was.

If Danika and Cliona ever wanted to try and see if this thing between them might work, Cliona had to see her, all of her, and be okay with all her parts.

Danika hadn't missed the heat in Cliona's gaze as Danika sang, hadn't missed the way that Cliona had shifted in her seat, and had Cliona stuck around long enough for Danika to try and speak to her again, Danika would have asked her if that charged eye contact had turned Cliona on as much as it had Danika.

It had been late afternoon by the time Danika had surfaced from her bed, her headache mostly gone, but the melancholy was something she found harder to shift. She'd texted Oli to ask if they wanted dinner, that she was gonna cook something, and that she could make enough for everyone if Jameson and Sinéad wanted to eat as well.

Danika wasn't the best cook, but she could make a mean spaghetti Bolognese. Once Oli texted back to say they would love dinner, she asked him to grab some mince on the way home while she rooted in the fridge for mushrooms and onions, and thankfully found a big jar of sauce in the cupboard.

Making herself a coffee, Danika went back upstairs to take a shower, trying to wash off the remainder of her hangover. She then dressed in sweatpants, and a loose t-shirt. Heading back down to the kitchen after towel drying her hair, Danika had just stepped into the kitchen when her phone rang.

Hoping it was Cliona, Danika took it out of her pocket and let out a groan as she saw her mother's name flashing on the screen.

If there was anything Danika hated more than dealing with her mother, it was dealing with her mother when she was hungover as fuck.

Danika prepared herself mentally for having to deal with Siobhan Keane, then pressed answer on the phone, switching it to loudspeaker. "Hello, Mother."

"Why are you not answering Bruno's phone calls?"

Danika rolled her eyes. Of course, Bruno would have called Siobhan, knowing full well that she would ring her daughter from wherever her current cruise ship was floating the moment Bruno called her to say that Danika wasn't behaving.

"Because Bruno is a pain in the ass and I'm on vacation."

"Danika, darling, we are performers. We do not take vacations."

Danika huffed out some air. Considering Siobhan was living her life on a constant vacation, she wasn't one to preach. Not that Danika would ever say that to her mother.

"Mam, I have things I need to be doing, so can you conclude this lecture of how I'm living my life so horribly and get to the point."

"Danika Keane!" Her mother said in a horrified tone, "You do not get to speak to your mother like this. I carried you for nine months, I gave up my figure and my career for you. I am not one of your minions you get to speak down to."

Danika had never spoken down to anyone who worked with her. And her mother spoke often about how being pregnant with Danika had robbed her of her career, and her figure. Siobhan also seemed to forget that Oli's mam's illness had also put a halt to her pop career, but Danika would shoulder the blame if only so that Siobhan didn't bring it up to Oli.

The front door opened, and Oli came in carrying a shopping bag, with Niamh, Jameson, and Sinéad bringing up the rear. Oli pointed at the phone and Danika put her finger to her head as if it was a gun and pressed, and Oli grinned, knowing who was on the other end.

"Hello, second mammy."

"Oliver, my sweet boy."

Oli shoved at Danika when she rubbed her temples. Siobhan would have much preferred to have a boy like Oli, than a girl like her. Thankfully, as scatty as Siobhan was, once this call was over, it would probably be a couple of months before she remembered to call Danika again.

"How is the cruise ship life? Are you breaking the hearts of all those pervy old men?"

Siobhan laughed. "Oh Oliver, I do miss your sense of humour. It's such a shame it never rubbed off on your sister."

Danika gave the phone her middle finger, then dove into the shopping bag for the mince so she could start cooking. The others had taken a seat at the table, looking at Danika and Oli as Siobhan started to talk again. "Oliver, my love, if Danika is being a pest, just kick her out. I'm sure she doesn't want to be an inconvenience while she is on vacation."

There was something in her mother's tone that Danika could almost hear the air quotes on the vacation. The humour vanished from Oli's face, and he must have seen the hurt on Danika's. Danika just carried on with her preparation of dinner, keeping her gaze away from the others. If she ever needed a reality check on just how insignificant her being a multimillion-selling artist was, her mam would be right there to provide it.

"Dani has been great. She's been keeping Niamh company while I've had a few things on. I love having my sister here with me, and Dani is always welcome in my home."

Siobhan snorted, and with her next comment, Danika knew that Siobhan had no clue anyone else was listening in. "I'm sure the mother of your child will get tired of the Oli and Dani show after a few weeks."

To Danika's surprise, it was Niamh who answered, the woman smiling as she said, "Actually, as someone who has a very close relationship with my own brother, I would never get tired of having Danika around. Oli and Danika know she is welcome here for as long as we can keep her here."

Silence on the other end of the line for a heartbeat before Siobhan said, "Danika, call Bruno so he stops annoying me. I will speak to you soon. Goodbye Oliver, darling."

The call ended then as Danika just went on with her cooking. Siobhan had a way of getting under her skin, making her feel inadequate. She threw the meat into the pot and added some seasoning and a stock cube when it was browned.

"Danika?"

She glanced over her shoulder at Niamh. "I meant what I said. Our door is always open to family."

Danika was grateful, her throat thick with emotion as she went back to her cooking. The others chatted away to themselves, and it wasn't long before Danika was serving up the meal, though her appetite was gone. Danika herself toyed with her meal until Jameson cleared his throat.

"Rhys is still pinching himself after last night. He's not gonna forget that in a long while."

"I'm going mad I missed it. And I missed seeing Oli and Danika perform together."

Oli leaned over and kissed Niamh's cheek. "Next time. I forgot how much I missed being on stage with Dani. We haven't done that since the night of the school showcase."

Danika shrugged, stabbing at her pasta as she blurted out. "I think I'm gonna go back to London."

The silence around the table weighed down on Danika, and she expected Oli to argue with her, and he opened his mouth to do just that when Niamh rested her hand on Oli's arm. Danika felt like that was their way of letting her go, but then Jameson spoke.

"Well, I was hoping you'd stick around for a little while longer. Wanted to see if you were serious about featuring on our next album."

Danika jerked her head toward Jameson and felt her cheeks heat. "I've already been working on something."

"So have I. Dec said to follow it through and since we are kinda family, we could spend some time working on it, and see where it goes. If you're sticking around that is."

Danika glanced over at Oli, and her best friend just said. "Stay."

So, Danika decided to stay...for now.

CHAPTER SEVENTEEN

Danika

THERE HAD BEEN TOO many thoughts swirling around in Danika's head that had made it impossible to sleep. Despite the residual feelings after her mother's phone call, Danika had enjoyed the rest of the night hanging with Oli, Niamh, Jameson, and Sinéad. It was only when Niamh said that Cliona had texted to say she would call over the following evening that Danika's stomach churned, and a nervousness fluttered in her pulse.

When they had all gone to bed, with Jameson and Sinéad taking one of the other spare rooms, Danika had lain awake for hours, unable to fall asleep. After tossing and turning for a good few hours, Danika had decided to just get the hell up and go for a run.

The cold air had burned her lungs as she ran, the

music in her ears calming her as her feet tore up the road. Danika felt so much better after her run, turning off her earbuds as she walked into the house, and it was then she heard the raised voices.

"You fucking kept it from me, Niamh! I had to find out from some journo who was delighted by my dumb as fuck face when he told me."

Woah...Oli hardly ever raised his voice, and right now, he sounded like he was fit to commit murder.

"Oli, I was gonna tell you, but there was never a right time."

Danika heard Oli snort, and was about to head upstairs and let them have their privacy, but then she heard Oli say. "Like you weren't gonna tell me about the baby?"

Danika headed straight for the kitchen at the sound of Niamh's sharp intake of breath. "That's a low blow, Oli. That was different and I thought we had gotten past it."

Entering the kitchen, Danika took in the scene. Niamh and Oli were standing on opposite sides of the kitchen counter. Oli's face was twisted in rage, his hands gripping the edge of the counter like he wanted to break it. Niamh looked crestfallen, her hand on her belly, like she needed the comfort. She was only wearing silk pyjama pants and one of Oli's tees, and Oli only had on shorts.

"Ya, well so did I. But then I find out from a jour-nalist that you and your ex have been texting each other because he's hoping to win you back. What was it the journo said? That Brian was willing to overlook the fact that you were having another man's baby because he loved you that much!"

Danika paused to look at Niamh, her eyes shimmering with the tears she was trying not to shed as she argued with Oli. Noticing that Danika was in the room, Oli turned and growled at her.

"Mind your own fucking business, Danika."

"You made it my business when you are shouting loud enough to give the paparazzi outside your gate an exclusive story for the afternoon edition. Take it down a notch, Oli."

"Fuck off."

"Oli," Niamh said as she held up her hands, "Did Brian text me out of the blue and invite me to dinner? Yes. But I told him that I had no desire to go backwards, and I was happy. That my family was my only priority."

Oli threw his hands up in the air. "If that's the truth, then why the fuck is Brian telling everyone who will goddamn listen that you and him are in contact all the time, and would be meeting for dinner soon? I swear to God, Niamh, you are not going to dinner with him."

Danika glanced at Niamh and saw the flicker of anger in her eyes. "You do not get to order me around, Oliver Scott. I love you but you do not own me. I have no intention of seeing Brian, but that is MY fucking choice, and not yours. Don't you dare pull that masochistic crap with me because I won't stand for it. Are you listening to me?"

Jameson and Sinéad had come down the stairs and Danika held up a hand to stop them from coming into the kitchen and adding to the tension. Jameson frowned but did what she asked as Oli leaned forward on the counter.

"I hear you loud and clear. But you don't get to lie to me about things that directly affect me. You've been lying to me for fucking weeks, and now that complete asshole is walking around telling everyone that you are running back to him. How the hell do you think that makes me look? Pathetic...and fucking easily discarded!"

Oli's voice had risen as he had spoken, but Oli's anger suddenly made sense to Danika. He wasn't really angry at Niamh; he was damn near terrified that the woman he loved was gonna leave him and take his baby with her. Danika heard it loud and clear in his voice.

"I think that's enough, Oli," Jameson said as she came in to stand beside Niamh.

Oli laughed, his hands balling into fists. "I'm not sick this time, Jay. You don't get to beat up a defense-less man this time."

Danika had heard fucking enough. She strode over to Oli, who stepped back, and she put her hands on his bare chest, shoving him hard. Oli focused on her then, dragging his eyes away from Niamh and Jameson.

"Go and cool the fuck down because the moment your brain catches up with your mouth, you'll be fucking sorry for the stupid shit that you've just sprouted." When Oli made to argue with Danika, she shoved him again and quirked a brow.

With a growl of frustration, Oli pivoted around and strode out the back, the sliding door slamming and then Danika heard him scream "fuck", in the same aggressive tone as he did when he was on stage. Then he just sat down on the grass and held his head in his hands. Danika was torn between going to comfort her best friend and explaining what had just happened.

"Jesus, I never knew Oli had a temper like that," Jameson said, and Danika was already shaking her head.

"He doesn't. He's not angry, Niamh. He's terrified."

Niamh looked confused as Danika set her ear pods on the counter. "Everyone Oli has loved has left him in some way. His mam to her illness. His dad after his mam tried to drown him. The only two people that haven't left him is me and JJ. And believe me that's not for want of trying. He pushed us away too, at the start, but we stayed."

Danika saw Niamh's eyes flicker in understanding, so Danika went on. "He loves you and that baby more than Oli has ever loved anything in his life. More than music. And that little boy who lost both of the people who were supposed to love him unconditionally, is telling Oli that he's gonna lose you too."

Niamh rested her hand on her heart. "Oh Oli. I didn't mean to lie to him, I just didn't think it was worth dragging up the past. Brian is so insignificant in all of this. I love Oli. I'd never leave him."

Danika held up her hands. "I know. But before anyone has a go at him, let his brilliant brain make sense of things in his head, and let him apologise. He'll feel better for it."

They all turned round at the sound of the patio door sliding open. Oli looked devastated. He ran his hand through his hair, his eyes on Niamh as he said. "I'm sorry. Can we talk?"

Niamh nodded her head and stepped around the counter to do to him. Sinéad sucked in a breath, as she passed by Jameson and Danika heard her tell him to call for an ambulance. Then was suddenly standing in front of Niamh, her hands resting on the other woman's shoulders. Niamh looked at her future sister-in-law in surprise.

"Niamh, I don't want you to panic, and do not look down, but you are bleeding. Jameson is calling an ambulance. You need to stay calm right now, okay?"

Despite the reassuring tone in Sinéad's voice, it was hard not to see the panic in both Niamh and Oli's eyes. Hell, even Danika was freaked out when Sinéad stepped away and Danika saw the blood staining Niamh's pyjama bottoms.

"Oli"

Oli went straight to Niamh and took her in his arms, kissing her forehead. "I've got you. I've got you both."

Jameson, who had gone out to call an ambulance, came back in. "Ambulance is like an hour out. There was a five-car crash on the Dunkettle Roundabout."

Niamh let loose a sob, as Oli snatched his car keys off the counter. "Fuck that. I'll drive there faster. Jameson, can you come and sit with Niamh?"

Niamh's brother nodded, then wrapped an arm around Niamh as he led her out, Oli already starting up the car, and then they were gone and all Danika could think was she hoped that mini Scott was a fighter like their parents', because if Niamh lost the baby, Oli would never forgive himself.

Chapter Eighteen

Cliona

LIONA GLANCED at the clock on the wall for like the hundredth time in the space of the last half hour, and yet, time seemed to be going excruciatingly slowly. She tried to distract herself from her nervousness about going to Niamh's for dinner, of seeing Danika again, by spending the afternoon in the bookshop rearranging shelves. She had always found it kinda soothing, the process of clearing and rearranging books.

And Cliona had spent a lot of time thinking about Danika. Part of her wanted to throw caution out the window and take the rockstar to bed. However, Cliona wanted more than just a hot, sexy, one-night stand. She had thought she had found that with Dani, but could she have it with Danika?

It had heated Cliona's cheeks to think of how

turned on she had been by Danika when she performed, and it had taken some alone time in bed to stroke herself to release, Danika's name on her lips as she came apart. Though Cliona had wished it was Danika's fingers thrusting inside of her as she orgasmed.

A customer came around the corner into the alcove then, dragging Cliona from her thoughts. Cliona found the graphic novel that he was looking for, then went back to her sorting. She didn't know how long she got lost in her work, but when she was working on a lower shelf, sat on the ground, Cliona heard a throat clear, and she jerked to attention, whirling around and her mouth almost gaped open.

Danika stood at the corner of the alcove, her expression guarded, but Cliona ran her gaze over Danika, and licked her lips. Intense blue eyes tracked the flicker of her tongue, as Danika folded her arms under her chest, pushing her cleavage up in the black vest that had Cliona wondering how they would feel if she cupped them in her grasp.

Her arms were bare, showing off the tattoo on her upper arm. She wore loose combats that seemed to be something Danika liked to wear, the waist hung low on her hips, showing off her midriff and the piercing at her navel. She wore no makeup, her hair pulled back into a braid showcasing her sharp angles and haunting blue eyes.

No matter how many times Cliona laid eyes on

Danika Kean, she would always be struck by just how shockingly beautiful she was.

"Hey," Danika said, her tone even...cautious.

Cliona got up off the ground, dusting off her jeans, then offered Danika a small smile. "Hey yourself. I thought Oli was coming to get me for dinner? And it's seriously early...Nessa won't be here for a little while."

Danika leaned against the wall. "Niamh asked me to come in person and explain why she had to cancel dinner at the last minute. She's okay now, but Niamh had some bleeding this morning, so Oli and Jameson took her to the hospital."

Cliona must have looked panicked because Danika's face softened. "Niamh and mini Scott are okay. Apparently, all that dancing my niece or nephew has been doing caused some sort of tear and that's why Niamh was bleeding. Doc said it was something that happens sometimes with active babies. She's being kept in overnight just to keep an eye on her blood pressure, so she wanted me to come and tell you she was okay in person so you wouldn't worry."

Releasing the breath that she hadn't realized she was holding; Cliona rubbed at her sternum to try and release the punch of panic that had taken root in her chest. "Thank God. Poor Niamh. She must have been so frightened. And Oli too."

Something crossed over Danika's expression that made Cliona want to press the rockstar for a little bit more information. And yet, Cliona didn't push too hard as Danika reached up and played with the ends of her braid.

"Listen, I wanted to clear the air about what happened the other night."

"Which part?" Cliona asked, bending down to pick up a book and place it back on the shelf.

"The part where I tried too hard to show you what you were missing. It was a bit much."

There was an edge of sadness in Danika's tone, but Cliona had seen it the way that Danika had intended her performance. She had been truthful with Cliona, and she had appreciated it, if it both scared and aroused her at the same time.

Shaking her head, Cliona responded to Danika. "Don't apologize. It was the most honest thing you could have done. I knew, *I know* that you are this uber-famous rockstar, Danika. You reminded me of that. I finally see all the parts of you. I get that Dani and Danika are the same woman. It was just hard for me to believe it to begin with."

"But it doesn't make you want to give us a shot?" Danika asked her, a sadness in that husky tone of hers that had Cliona wanting her to hear it when they were naked.

"I'm not sure," Cliona admitted, running a hand through her hair. "I knew when we were talking in the beginning that you lived in London and thought, ya, I can go over and see you when I have a few days here and there, but Danika, what happens when you go on tour and spend three months in a different city, every day?"

Danika pressed her tempting lips into a firm line. "Well, though it's not the point, but it would be another year or so before I tour again to far-off places. I need to sort contract things and get my new album sorted, and I might do that here. But after that, Cliona, if I had to go on the road for a while, we would work something out. Have you never wanted to see the world?"

Had she? It had never struck her as something that was obtainable for Cliona to do. Her life had been all about finding stability, to ensuring she had a good job and a roof over her head. That had been her plan, her goal. Travelling around the globe with a rockstar girl-friend was not something Cliona could have ever imagined.

But it took more than words to just wipe away any reservations that Cliona might have. Niamh was in the spotlight now as much as Oli was, and Cliona didn't know if she was built for that.

"I'm not sure what's going on in your head, but you can't deny that the chemistry between us is insane. I'm not a masochist, so if you can't see past what I do for a living, I won't push anymore. We can be friends." Danika said the word friends like she had smelled something rotten, those blue eyes on her as Cliona saw the corners of Danika's mouth kick up.

"Maybe I should give you something else to think about."

Danika strode toward her, even as Cliona backed herself up against one of the bookcases. Reaching out, Danika slid her hand around the back of Cliona's neck, tilting her head upwards, her thumb beneath her chin. The possessive touch made Cliona's legs tremble, her body heating as Danika pressed herself up against her, breasts flush as Cliona drew in some air.

Then Danika's lips were brushing against Cliona's before teeth grazed her bottom lip. Cliona's heart was beating so loud she couldn't concentrate, then Danika's other hand gripped Cliona's hip, and any control Cliona had disappeared.

But there was no denying that Danika would be the more dominant partner in bed as she pressed Cliona harder into the bookcase, the shelf digging into her back as Danika licked along the seam of Cliona's lips and Cliona reached her own hands out to rest on Danika's ribs.

The press of Danika's soft, firm lips intensified and from one heartbeat to the next, the kiss went from chaste to red hot. Danika plunged her tongue into Cliona's mouth, their teeth almost banging, then Danika pressed her thigh between Cliona's legs and she felt like she was about to come apart.

Danika devoured her mouth like she was famished, and Cliona was only too happy to let her work out whatever tension she obviously had. Cliona kissed Danika back, and felt the other woman's moan vibrate against her lips, Cliona was certain that if Danika stripped her naked, right here and now, Cliona would let her.

Books fell to the floor, and Cliona faintly heard Molly call out and ask if Cliona was okay.

Then Danika broke the kiss, taking a step back, her chest heaving, and Cliona was in the same condition as she called out to Molly that everything was fine. There was absolutely no way after a kiss like that, a kiss that was life-affirming and defining, that she and Danika could ever be just friends.

Cliona took a step toward Danika, who just offered Cliona a smile, a smile that was smug and teasing at the same time as Danika said. "Now just imagine how much better it would feel to have my tongue fucking your pussy."

CHAPTER NINETEEN

Danika

DANIKA WAS IN A TERRIBLE MOOD.

After one hell of a kiss at Rebel Books, Danika had just walked out to leave Cliona to think over her parting words, but since then, radio silence. Danika had been checking her phone constantly, and it pissed her off that even after that kiss, Cliona wasn't blowing up her phone.

But if Cliona was all over you, would you be as interested in her as you are?

As much as Oli felt unnerved when Danika was the voice of reason, Danika hated it even more when she was the voice of reason to herself. Of course, with her track record, which was way worse than Oli's, Danika couldn't blame Cliona for being cautious.

Even if it frustrated the hell out of Danika.

Danika had busied herself with making sure Niamh would be able to chill when she got out of the hospital. She'd gone shopping, had bought the tea Niamh liked, chocolate and ice cream, and enough food to feed them all for a month. She had also popped into Penny's to get Niamh some new pyjamas and slippers, and even a fleecy blanket. And then had gone and spent an insane amount of money on things for the baby.

A big bouquet of flowers had arrived shortly after Danika had gotten back to Niamh and Oli's from JJ, and the exquisite flowers came already in a fancy vase, so Danika set them on the counter. She then texted her other brother, asking why he never sent her flowers, laughed out loud when JJ sent back a text to say Danika wasn't the flowers kind of girl, and he had already sent some Hot Topic tees in the mail to her.

The front door opened, and Danika sprang into action, turning on the kettle as Niamh and Oli came into the house.

"Oli, stop fussing. The doctor said I'm okay. That the baby is okay."

"Stop snarling at me woman and just let me look after you both. Please."

Danika grinned as Niamh came into the kitchen, and rolled her eyes when Danika started fussing over her too. Niamh lowered herself down on the couch with a sigh, kicked off her shoes, and then rested her hands on her stomach.

"Since you two are fussing about, can I get one of you to make me a sandwich, please?"

Danika finished making Niamh's tea, as Oli made her a sandwich. Grabbing the new blanket that she'd bought for Niamh; Danika lay it over Niamh's legs. Niamh took Danika's hand in hers and gave it a squeeze. "Thank you."

With a shrug of her shoulders, Danika replied. "I noticed you have a shit ton of blankets around the gaff. Saw it and just said *why not*? Also, I may have gone overboard and bought my niece or nephew way too much stuff."

"You didn't have to do that, Danika, but thank you."

Danika smiled at Niamh. "Auntie Dani had to be the first person to buy him or her their first pair of Air Jordans."

Oli laughed at that, and knew Danika had a thing for sneakers as he came over and handed Niamh her sandwich. His face was pale, and he looked like he hadn't slept in days, even though it was only just over twenty-four hours. Danika asked Oli if he wanted some food, but he just shook his head, resting his head on Niamh's shoulder, and closed his eyes.

It didn't take long for her friend to fall asleep, and Danika got up, grabbed another blanket, and placed it over Oli. Then she took the plate from Niamh so as not to disturb Oli, who was out like a light.

"You want me to wake him so you can move?" Danika asked, but Niamh only smiled.

"Nah, he's been stressed and riddled with guilt after yesterday. Though, he only has about twenty minutes before I'll need to pee so he might as well enjoy it."

That last part made Danika chuckle as she sat down beside Niamh, and rested her head on the other shoulder, making Niamh laugh softly as Oli threw an arm over to rest a hand on her stomach. Danika didn't want to pry about how they had come to resolve things between them, however, Niamh seemed to sense the question because she began to speak in a low voice.

"Oli was blaming himself for what happened, but it was just one of those things. Not that I wasn't scared. I was fucking terrified. After we found out that everything was okay with Mini Scott, we talked, and we both made mistakes. I told him what you said, and he told me that you were right, even if it was annoying to admit."

Danika smiled as she curled her legs underneath her. "I think that's why he kept me around. We call each other out on our bullshit. JJ's the same. Oh, by the way, the over-the-top flowers are from him. Flashy fucker."

Niamh snorted, then rested her hand over Oli's hand on her stomach. "I can't imagine what it was like for him, to be abandoned by Arthur so soon after what happened with his mam. My family have always been so close, that it's hard to make sense of it. After Layla died, it cemented the closeness, even if we were mainly focused on keeping Jameson sane. I'm glad Oli had you, then JJ. And that our baby will have all of these people to look after him or her."

"No matter where life takes us, that's never gonna be in doubt. And I'm gonna give you two some space."

Niamh made to argue, but Danika lifted her head and looked at Niamh. "I'm gonna hang with Jameson tonight and work on that song for my album. He called me this morning and said Sinead and Shay are having a girl's night, and Rhys is hanging with Andi and Dec. We have the studio to ourselves so gonna take advantage of it."

Danika leaned back in her seat, as Niamh questioned. "But that means you'll be staying around here, right?"

Danika shrugged. "Maybe. I haven't worked out the details yet, but I do need to have a serious conversation with Oli. Don't stress yourself. His answer will mean me staying in Ireland on a more permanent basis or heading back to the UK by my lonesome."

"Well, maybe you could at least hang around for the next month or so until the baby arrives. Something tells me Oli's gonna be worrying and he needs his little sister to keep his head on straight."

Danika chuckled this time. "Two months I can totally agree to. Plus, I need to be here to bond with the baby so Uncle JJ doesn't swoop in with his Hollywood looks and stupid face and charm the baby. I have to establish myself as the favourite aunt, yano."

Niamh laughed, then winced. "Shit. I really need to pee after that kick."

The other woman reached over and gently shook Oli's shoulder. "Oli, wake up a second."

Oli darted upright; his eyes wide as he stared at Niamh. "Are you okay? Is it the baby?"

Niamh patted his cheek affectionately. "We are both okay, I promise. My bladder not so much. Lemmie go pee and then maybe we could curl up in bed and get some sleep? I just want to get under our duvet and lock out the world for a little while."

Oli's smile was bright, even if his eyes were tired, "Anything you want, gorgeous. Anything at all."

Danika watched as Oli helped Niamh to her feet, and then she walked out to the bathroom as Oli turned to look back at Danika. She rolled her eyes before saying. "I'm heading out to meet up with Jameson to work on some music. Go get some rest, Oli, you look like shit."

Oli didn't laugh. He simply just said. "I love you, Dani."

Danika grinned as she lowered her voice to make sure Niamh didn't hear. "I know. I love you too, you soppy git. And just so you know, I think that ring would look better on Niamh's finger than it does in the box. Think about that."

Oli didn't reply to her statement, just went to help

Niamh to bed so Danika tidied up the plates and stuff, before she headed out to meet Jameson at the studio, leaving the couple to some peace in their own home.

It would be good for Danika to get down to some work, to take her mind off of Oli, Niamh, and especially off of Cliona. She needed a few hours of focus to get herself back in balance, back on equal footing. She could lose herself in the lyrics, in the words and the melody and not focus on the fact her private life was slowly imploding. Her work life might not be in a much better condition, but Danika knew that she needed to figure out where the next stage in her career was headed, and at least she had control over that.

Even if she only started with one song, it was a start.

CHAPTER TWENTY

Danika

DANIKA WAS ALREADY FEELING ten times better as she strummed the strings of the acoustic guitar that Jameson had loaned her. Jameson was sitting across from her, his own guitar in his grasp. They were both sitting on the floor, legs stretched out, though Danika had laughed at how short hers looked compared to Jameson's long limbs.

They had notes scattered all over the place, sheets of music too, but in the chaos, they had actually started to put together a decent song. Danika had been surprised at how good Jameson's voice was, and even though she had listened to the song he had written about losing his first love Layla, it had been a pleasant discovery to realize that his voice had an edge to it that Danika liked.

They'd stopped to eat some pizza and drink a beer or two, with Jameson telling Danika that Sinéad would drop her back to Oli's when she came to pick Jameson up after her girl's night. That had made Danika smile, though a sharp ache found its way to her chest. Jameson had asked her what the matter was, and Danika had just shrugged.

"I was just thinking it must be nice to have a place to call home, and someone to come home to."

Jameson took a drink of his beer as he balanced his guitar on his leg. "Is that what you want, Danika?"

Danika felt uncomfortable at Jameson's question, so just shrugged. Jameson set his beer down, then played a few chords as he said, "If that's what you want, then go out and find it. When Layla died, I never expected to be able to love again and then I met Sinéad. I was shattered on the inside, didn't want anyone to see me and know that I was more than a little broken. But Sinéad didn't care. She knows how much Layla means to me, and she never makes me feel bad for thinking about her."

Jameson glanced away for a second, then he looked back at Danika. "I wasn't keen on moving in with Sinéad, the thought of loving and losing her made me afraid to commit, but going home to her was worth the gamble. And I can't wait to marry her, whenever we can set a date that doesn't clash with everyone else's plans."

That had made Danika laugh, knowing that Jameson's friends were in the marrying stage of their lives, and with the crazy lives they lived, getting everyone together must be hell.

They'd gone back to working on the song then, the time slipping by. The song had ended up more rock than goth, but since the song was gonna be on Heartache Melody's album, Danika didn't mind. It made her think of how she could totally do an album that was still her, but more rock than emo...considering she was now more of an Elder Emo than a Goth Princess.

Danika tested some chords for the pre-chorus, and her and Jameson singing the lyrics together.

> *Life's a bitch,*
> *and you hate it when I cry,*
> *life's a bitch,*
> *and I hate it when you lie.*

"It would be great if we had Luna do something with the drums in between the cry and the next life's a bitch. Like amping up the tension."

Danika nodded, making a note of that on the sheet music she had with the lyrics on it. "Once we get shit nailed down, we defo need to loop in the rest of the band and see what ideas they come up with. But with a heavy drum in the background, it will sound very angsty."

They kept working on it and were so deep in

concentration that they didn't notice Declan coming in until he flopped down on the chair across from them. Both Danika and Jameson just inclined their heads and went back to working put the lyrics.

Careful not to disturb them, Danika approved of how Declan just sat back and studied them both, a smile curving his lips as they tossed ideas back and forth. Danika was surprised with how easy it was to work with Jameson, considering she normally wrote songs, and then sent them to Oli to have a look at before she started to record anything seriously.

Danika might just have another ear to bend when she was stuck on a track, when Oli was taking time to be the dad he deserved to be. Lifting her gaze to Declan, who was just reclined in the chair happy to listen to them, Danika asked him to sing a few bars.

She handed Declan the lyrics as she played the chords on the guitar. Declan's gravelly tone almost suffocated the melody, and Danika frowned, knowing it didn't sound quite right.

Jameson must have heard it too because he barely looked up as he stated. "Nah, Dec...try it like this."

Jameson sang a few bars as Danika joined in, and then it dawned on Danika that the song didn't suit Declan's voice. The song didn't need Declan's graveled tone, it needed an easier, unexpected voice, and from the glint in Declan's eyes, he had come to the same conclusion.

"I don't think it works with me singing it, lads."

Declan glanced over at Jameson. "You should sing it with Danika, Jay."

Jameson's eyes went wide, a flush in cheeks, even if his eyes already gave away how badly he wanted to do it. The song was as much his as it was Danika's. "I can't do that."

"Sure you can. And from the grin on Danika's face, she's all on board with that. The song needs a less aggressive tone and you two sing well together. Better than well. Annoyingly so, but Danika can't steal you so you can form some super duo. Plus no one is gonna fuckin expect this. And the fans will love it."

Jameson looked like he was in shock. "Rhys could do it."

Declan leaned forward. "There is no way Rhys would turn down the opportunity to sing with Danika, but we both know, Jay, if you say no now, you'll regret it for the rest of your life. You know you can sing. You have what it takes to make this a hit song. You and Danika. I'm happy to take over guitar duties for ya. This is your song, yours and Danika's."

Jameson looked at Danika, but she was already buzzing with excitement. Holding out her fist, Danika waited as Jameson bumped her knuckles, and then they were all grinning. Declan reached out and motioned for Jameson to hand over his guitar, and Danika handed him the sheet music.

Declan played the chords over and over until he no longer needed the sheet music. Jameson got to his feet and paced, but Danika started to sing, then Jameson joined in and then Danika was on her feet, walking back and forth as things took even more shape.

That was what they were doing when Sinéad and Shay showed up, then Andi and Rhys. Jumping right on the keyboard, Rhys was quick to pick it up, and Danika knew that this would be a massive hit.

As everyone made to head out, Danika set her borrowed guitar on the couch, and then looked at Jameson. "We should rope Oli in to direct the music video. He always comes up with some amazing shit."

"You trying to make up for the fact that you two haven't done a song yet?" Declan asked with a chuckle as he slung an arm around Andi's shoulder.

"He never asked me. One day but musically, me and Oli are in two different places. I don't think a song we wrote together would gel as much as this one with Jameson." Danika replied honestly.

"Maybe. But we made Never Back Down work."

"True," Danika conceded, as she walked outside into the early morning light. "Though that was an all-out rager of a song. Oli just had to do what he always does. Even I wouldn't have fit on that track."

Andi rolled her eyes, then yawned. "Hey, we need to talk about doing a press release about you signing up with Rebel PR soon. Have you told the record label yet that you don't want to resign with them? I need to get ahead of the evitable questions."

Danika laughed as she rolled her eyes, getting into

the back of Sinéad's car as she waved at Andi and Declan, then Rhys and Shay. Sitting back in her seat, Danika glanced out the window as Jameson asked Sinéad how her girl's night went.

Today had been a good day, in the end, and Danika found that even though she had a life, had a career in London, the longer she stayed in Ireland, in Cork, the more London seemed like it was far away. Danika spent a lot of time alone in London, and fake smiling at shitty events she didn't want to be at. Here, Danika had family, and new friends that didn't care that she was Danika Keane, she was just one of them. Perhaps, like Oli, the reason why she had no permanent home was because no place had ever felt like home to Danika.

Chapter Twenty-One

Cliona

CLIONA WALKED through the gates having gotten out of her taxi and headed to the door of Niamh and Oli's house having waved at one of the security guys Oli had employed to keep an eye on the house. She wasn't sure why she was so nervous.

No, that was a lie.

That kiss. That earth-shattering, life-altering kiss made her nervous. The way the kiss had made her feel even before the dirty promise in Danika's words. *"Now just imagine how much better it would feel to have my tongue fucking your pussy."*

Cliona hadn't known what to say in response to that even when Danika had strode out the door without so much as a glance back at her. It had taken a solid thirty minutes before her heart finally slowed down.

Honestly, if it had been up to Cliona, she would have avoided seeing Danika again for a while until she could make sense of the feelings swirling inside of her. But Sorcha had asked her if she could drop over some papers for Niamh to look over because she had to go out to her parent's farm to deal with something.

So now Cliona was standing with her hand on the door, trying to decide if she should just post the papers through the letterbox or leave them with the security guy. Letting out a sigh, Cliona knocked, then twisted the handle downward.

Stepping inside, Cliona could hear music coming from somewhere in the massive house, but the kitchen was empty. Cliona set the papers down on the counter, and called Niamh's name. When she didn't get a response, Cliona found herself following the sound of the piano that was being played.

She walked up the curved staircase that would have been at home in a period show, then down the hallway. Her pulse began to race as she neared the room where the most beautiful music was coming from.

Stepping through the open door, Cliona's mouth fell open at the chaos inside the room. Sheets of music were thrown all over the floor. Musical instruments were placed in different spots. Cliona glanced down to the side to see a Heartache Melody t-shirt discarded, and she followed the path of discarded clothes to the beautiful woman who was also thrown on the floor.

Danika Keane lay on her stomach, wearing nothing but a pair of black lace boy shorts and a matching bra. Her black hair was loose around her shoulders as she tinkered with a keyboard in front of her. She had a pen tucked behind one ear, another in her grasp. She had headphones on, her shoulders moving in time with the music she was playing on the keyboard.

Cliona couldn't stop herself from roaming her eyes over Danika. The curves that made Cliona's mouth water when Danika was dressed were on display to her. The generous curve of her ass and hips, the round firm breasts, the creamy skin on display. As the evening sun shone through the windows Cliona knew that even calling Danika a rockstar didn't adequately sum up who she was.

She looked more like a goddess, basking in the glory of sun and song.

As if Danika sensed someone in the room with her, she turned over and sat up, her eyes wide when she saw Cliona standing in the doorway. Cliona noted the hesitation in Danika's blue eyes as she removed her headphones. Cliona expected her to grab some clothes but Danika just leaned back on her arms, her hair falling back and her ample cleavage on display.

Cliona must have been staring because Danika

cleared her throat, Cliona's face heating as she tore her gaze from Danika.

"What are you doing here, Cliona?"

Ya, what was she doing here...oh ya, the papers for Niamh.

"Sorcha asked me to drop off some papers for Niamh."

"They're at the hospital," Danika replied, and when Cliona sucked in a breath, Danika shook her head. "She's grand. It's a normal check-up. But they won't be back for a couple of hours. I think Oli said something about Niamh's parents after the hospital but I wasn't really listening."

Cliona offered Danika a smile. "I guess you were in the zone."

"Ya, I was."

Danika's response had an edge to it, and Cliona thought it was because she had interrupted Danika's creativity. Swallowing hard, trying to not let herself feel disappointed because Cliona was the one who had been keeping her distance from Danika, Cliona took a step back.

"I'm sorry to interrupt you. Will you tell Niamh I came by?"

Danika slowly got to her feet, put her hands on her hips. Cliona could tell that Danika was a little pissed off, "That's all you got?"

Cliona sighed, not wanting another confrontation

with Danika. She opened her mouth to tell Danika just that when Danika got there first.

"I can't do this."

"Do what, Danika?" Cliona asked, and she heard the tremble in her own voice.

"I can't do this, this fucking animosity between us," Danika said in a flat tone that felt like a gut punch to Cliona. Danika was full of passion, full of life, and this dead tone was nothing like the Danika Cliona wanted so badly.

"I think I could be happy here. I think I could be less lonely here than I was in London. But with every step forward that I think I'm making with you, I might as well be in fucking Siberia. You know how much I want you. You know that I wanted to give this a shot, but I really can't keep making hurt because you don't want me."

Jesus, was that really what Danika thought...that Cliona didn't want her?

That wasn't the problem.

Cliona was scared. Scared of how she felt, scared of how much it would hurt if this thing with Danika ended badly. She might lose her friend. Cliona might lose the only people who had cared for her, and that terrified her.

But she never, ever, wanted Danika to think that Cliona didn't want her.

"I want you," Cliona heard herself say, her pulse

pounding so loud she could feel it in her ears, "I want you, Dani, more than anything I've ever wanted in my life. That's not the problem. This chemistry between us has never been the problem."

Cliona wanted to say more. She wanted to explain it all so Danika would know exactly what Cliona felt and her fears, and why it would be best if they tried to be friends. She didn't want Danika to feel lonely, because Cliona knew what it was like to feel lonely.

But Cliona never got the chance to say all those things.

Danika crossed the floor and took Cliona's face in her hands, kissed her hard on the lips. Cliona gasped, and Danika used that to plunge her tongue into Cliona's mouth. When Cliona knew she should have pushed Danika away, instead she kissed Danika back with a hunger that surprised her. Cliona lost herself in the kiss, in the feel of Danika, the passion that was fused into the DNA that was Danika. It was all consuming and everything Cliona had ever needed in her life.

Danika let go of Cliona's face to let her hands roam down Cliona's body, and then Cliona let loose a bark of laughter when Danika muttered that she was wearing far too many clothes. Danika kissed her again, swallowing her laughter, and this time, Danika began to pop open the buttons on Cliona's shirt.

"Dani, wait."

Danika's fingers halted and then Danika looked at her, and Cliona knew she wasn't gonna stop this. But Danika looked terrified that Cliona had changed her mind. Again.

This time, it was Cliona who leaned forward and she pressed her lisp to Danika's jaw. "I know that you and Oli are used to seeing each other naked and stuff, but I'm not too keen on having them walk in on us."

Cliona could feel Danika's smile as she kissed her cheek, then Danika grabbed her hand and dragged her from the room, down the hallway, and into another room that must be where Danika was staying; it smelt like her perfume in there. Danika closed the door and then continued to unbutton Cliona's shirt. Danika tossed it aside and then kissed down her throat, her lips blazing a trail until she kissed the swell of Cliona's breast. sucking hard enough that it made Cliona yelp.

Danika snapped her head up. "Shit, am I being too rough?"

Cliona cupped Danika's cheek. "No, I just wasn't prepared. It didn't hurt me just surprised me. I like having your lips on me, Dani."

That admission made Danika give her a smile that was seductive and smug at the same time. Cliona felt her heart kick like a drum inside her chest, as Danika slid a hand down Cliona's stomach, popping the button in Cliona's jeans without taking her eyes off Cliona.

"That's good," Danika said, her fingers working Cliona's zipper. "Because I plan on having my lips on each and every part of your body today. My hands too. And I'm gonna eat you like your pussy is my favourite dessert."

CHAPTER TWENTY-TWO

Danika

DANIKA HAD to try and rein herself in and not rush this with Cliona. Part of her wanted to take her time and savour the moment. But part of her was really motivated to get Cliona naked.

Less chance of her doing a runner if she was naked, right?

Casting that thought aside, Danika went back to her task. Slowly, she unzipped Cliona's pants, leaning in to press her lips to the skin just shy of her naval. Cliona sucked in a breath, then kicked off her shoes when Danika thumbed the loops of her jeans and slid them down over Cliona's slim hips.

Once Cliona's jeans were off and in a heap on the ground, Danika stole a kiss that dampened her already wet boy shorts. Cliona hadn't really even touched her yet and Danika was already on fire. Danika broke the kiss, and trailed her lips down Cliona's jaw, her neck, and back down to her breasts. Pressing a kiss to the swell of Cliona's breast, the other woman let out a very sexy moan as her head fell back against the door.

Danika pulled down the cup of Cliona's bra, then flicked her tongue over Cliona's taunt nipple. When Cliona shuddered, Danika did it again, then took as much of Cliona's breast into her mouth as possible and sucked. Cliona slapped her hands against the door as Danika continued to lick and suck her breast, and when Cliona wriggled, Danika switched to the other one.

Danika felt Cliona's fingers in her hair, the sting of the slight pull just making Danika feel hotter. Cliona pulled Danika's head up and kissed her, the first kiss that Cliona had initiated, and it took all of Danika's control not to take over.

She was used to being the one to take over in bed.

But she was fucking happy to let Cliona do wicked things to her if she wanted.

When they broke apart, they were both breathing a little heavier and then Cliona reached behind her to unclasp her bra, letting her breasts free for Danika to admire. She reached out and cupped Cliona's breasts, squeezing a little to see if Cliona could handle Danika a little rougher.

From the heat in Cliona's gaze, the answer was a resounding yes.

Reluctantly taking her hands off Cliona's breasts, Danika slid her hand down Cliona's body. Danika brushed two fingers along Cliona's damp panties, then dropped to her knees. Lifting her gaze up to Cliona's, Danika slid Cliona's panties down, letting her step out of them before she tossed them somewhere in the room.

Cliona laughed, the sensual sound turning to a moan when Danika ran her tongue along the inside of Cliona's thigh. Danika gently pushed Cliona's legs apart, gave Cliona a wicked smile, then made good on her promise.

Danika ate at Cliona like she had been starving and maybe she had been. After months of wanting, of needing Cliona like she had never needed anyone before, Danika poured it all into making Cliona see just how much she wanted her. Danika licked at her clit, sucked it, felt Cliona's legs tremble as her thighs pressed against the sides of Danika's head.

Sinking her tongue into Cliona's vagina, Danika moaned, the sound vibrating and adding to the pleasure Cliona was feeling. Danika licked and sucked and fucked Cliona until she slid her fingers into Danika's hair and tugged.

That only made Danika work a little faster and harder, then she felt Cliona's body tense before she ground out Danika's name and came against Danika's mouth. Slowing down the pace, Danika licked and sucked Cliona through her orgasm.

When Danika felt Cliona come down from her orgasm, she got to her feet and tugged Cliona toward the bed. She kissed Cliona until she got the other woman lying down on the bed, and then Danika took a step back.

Cliona was sprawled on Danika's bed, pushed up on her elbows watching Danika, her brown eyes wide. Her breasts rose with every inhalation and Danika thought she looked so fucking beautiful. Gods, Danika could get used to seeing Cliona naked in her bed.

Danika unclasped her bra from the front and then pushed down her shorts. The hunger in Cliona's eyes made her feel wanted. Desired. Danika was used to being wanted and desired by fans, by women who wanted a night with a rockstar, but Cliona was looking at her like she saw beyond the rockstar and wanted the woman Danika was.

Danika grinned, then crawled onto the bed. She straddled Cliona, letting loose a moan when their breasts were pressed together. They kissed, hands roaming freely over their skin, the feel of Cliona's touch leaving a blaze of heat burning Danika from the outside in.

Cliona hooked her leg around Danik's leg as Danika rubbed against Cliona's already slick core. The kissing grew hungrier, desperate even and Danika wanted to make Cliona come again.

Rolling them so that they lay side by side, Danika traced the fingers of her left hand down Cliona's face as she slid two fingers on her right hand into her mouth. Heat flared in Cliona's eyes.

They lay there, Danika on her left side, Cliona on her right for a few seconds before Danika nudged Cliona's legs apart with her knee, then didn't do anything for a minute.

"I want to spend the night making you come against my mouth. You taste so damn good, Cliona. More of that later. Now, I want to fuck you and be looking into your eyes when you come again, my name on your lips."

Cliona sucked in a breath as Danika sucked her fingers once more, then replaced her knee with her hand. Danika teased Cliona by rubbing her fingers along her slit before she slipped a finger inside of Cliona, the other woman wrapping her arms around Danika like she was afraid Danika was gonna stop.

Their bodies were pressed against one another, and after a few strokes of Danika's single digit, Danika added a second, and began to use faster strokes. Cliona clenched around her fingers, her eyes never leaving Danika's as she increased the tempo, then scissored her fingers, the sound of Cliona's husky moan like the sweetest melody to her ears.

Cliona's entire body tensed, and Danika knew that she was so close again. Looked like Cliona had a fast trigger and Danika was here for it. She grinned at Cliona and then said, "That's it, babe. Come for me while I'm fucking inside you."

Danika added a third finger, the pressure enough to push Cliona over the edge again. She kept her three fingers sliding in and out of Cliona, felt every tremor, every shudder, then slid her fingers all the way out to just stroke back in with two fingers until Cliona grabbed Danika's wrist.

"Just gimmie a minute."

Danika chuckled at the husky demand, and when Cliona let go of her wrist, Danika ran her hand up and down Cliona's body to rest on the curve of her ass. Cliona closed her eyes and leaned into the curve of Danika's neck. She was so still that Danika wondered if she had fallen asleep. Danika was okay with that because she wanted to sleep tangled up in Cliona and then wake her up with her mouth on her pussy.

Warm lips pressed against Danika's throat, and it added fuel to the inferno already inside her. She let out a moan as Cliona sucked hard enough on her throat that it might leave a mark. Danika fisted a hand in Cliona's hair, and yanked her up to capture Cliona's lips with her own.

Then Danika found herself on her back, Cliona pressed against her.

"Is it always this intense with you?" Cliona asked softly like she was afraid that speaking would break the spell between them.

Danika let her lips curve into a smile. "Guess you'll have to stick around and test that theory. I am more than motivated to be your test subject."

Cliona chuckled, and then her hands were cupping Danika's breasts. Rolling a nipple between her fingers, Danika arched into Cliona's touch. "Harder."

Arching a brow, Cliona hesitated before she pinched Danika's nipple. This time Danika was the one shuddering. Cliona palmed her breasts, simultaneously using her thumb and index finger to roll Danika's nipples and Danika let her head fall back against the pillow.

When Cliona flicked her tongue over Danika's already sensitive nipple, she jerked, her fingers digging into Cliona's ass, not that she seemed to mind. Their eyes locked. Cliona liked being the one to pleasure Danika. That was something she hadn't had much before. The women Danika had been with wanted to be the ones to be fucked by Danika.

But Cliona was looking at her, touching her like she wanted to be the one to make Danika come. Danika tightened her grip on Cliona's ass, the gorgeous woman giving Danika an almost shy smile as she leaned down to whisper in Danika's ear.

"Let's see if I can make you come as quickly as those sinful fingers and mouth made me."

Chapter Twenty-Three

Cliona

THE HEAT of the sun on her skin woke Cliona, as she came awake slowly. She was confused for a brief moment until the events of the night before all came flooding back to her. the feel of Danika's hands on her body, the touch, the taste, the mind-blowing orgasms. Her body ached from all of the pleasure and her heart; her foolish heart had already decided that it wanted to keep Danika.

So why the hell was she having a mini heart attack?

Darting upright in the bed, Cliona glanced down at Danika, who was sound asleep beside her. hair fanned out on the pillow, the duvet pushed down to over her lower half, Danika looked like a goddess bathed in sunlight. Cliona felt her palms itch as she remembered what it was like to cup those perfect handfuls and the sounds Danika had made when she tightened her grasp.

The moan that Damika had made when she had taken the peaks into her mouth and sucked had made her clit clench, pulse with an intensity that had almost short-circuited Cliona's brain.

Cliona was ruined now...because there would never be another woman like Danika Keane.

Quietly, Cliona slipped from the bed, threw on her discarded clothing, slipped out of the bedroom, and went to the bathroom before she tried to make an Irish exit before anyone realized that she had stayed over in Danika's bed.

She had made it all the way to the kitchen without any trouble, but what Cliona saw in the kitchen made her cheeks flush with a violent heat as she froze. Niamh was sitting on one of the stools by the counter, facing away, and she and Oli were making out. Then Oli was moving his mouth down Niamh's throat, and her friend let her head fall back with a groan.

Cliona couldn't stop herself from glancing down, and saw Oli's hand disappear under Niamh's night-dress. She really needed to get out of here before she could no longer look at her friend in the face ever again...or Oli.

Backing out of the kitchen, Cliona miscalculated where she was, and bumped into something hard that sent a dart of pain in her side. Her eyes went wide at the sound of the biggest crash she had ever heard in her life as glass shattered around her and there was no way of escaping without being seen.

Cliona heard Niamh let out a squeak, then Oli chuckled, before Cliona even dared lift her gaze to Niamh's as her friend said in a shocked tone, "Cliona?"

"Oh my god, I'm so sorry. I just wanted to leave, and no one be any the wiser but then you two were...and I um...shit. I'm just gonna go."

But Cliona was frozen unable to move as Niamh shifted off her seat, her own cheeks flushed but Cliona wasn't sure if it was in embarrassment like Cliona or .... well, yano.

"Wait, Cliona...did you stay over? With Danika?"

Oli was grinning as he came over to get down on his knees and pick up the glass that was around the place and put down a towel to soak up the water. Cliona didn't know what to do, as Niamh motioned for her to come over to her. Cliona glanced over her shoulder toward the stairs, then back at Niamh.

"I really need to go." Was all Cliona said quietly.

"At least have a coffee and something to eat before you go. Get the full B&B experience." Oli teased from where he was cleaning up, and that made Cliona blush even more than she already was.

"Oli, stop teasing her." Niamh chastised her rock-star, then came over to drag Cliona over to the couch. "You want to tell me what happened or do I have to go up and ask Danika."

Cliona shook her head, unsure what she could say to Niamh so that they would just let her leave. *I had earth-shattering sex with Danika, and now I'm freaked out and trying to do a runner. I want to go back upstairs and wake Danika up with my face between her legs, and her fingers in my hair.*

Cliona jerked to her feet, unable to say anything as Niamh's gaze narrowed. "Cliona, are you okay?"

No...she was far from okay...she was unravelling.

Cliona opened her mouth to respond, as Oli finished his cleanup, when Danika strode into the room, her hair all tousled, her eyes sleepy, and wearing nothing but a shirt that came down just below her thighs. She looked sexy as all hell and Cliona wanted another taste of her.

"She's just been rendered speechless by the absolutely fantastic sex. Best night's sleep I've had in ages. Cliona wore me out."

Cliona wanted the ground to open up and swallow her whole. She felt naked, exposed for all to see, and didn't know how Danika could so flippantly discuss their sex life like this.

Danika seemed oblivious to the way that Cliona was feeling, as she opened the fridge and looked inside. "Oli, I'm starving. Wanna help me cook up a fry? I know Niamh's always down for bacon."

Oli chuckled as Niamh perked up at the sound of a fry. Danika leaned back and her blue eyes locked with Cliona's, "You staying for breakfast?"

Cliona was already shaking her head as she surged forward and began to stumble over her words. "I have to, I mean, no, I have to ...leave...go...okay bye."

Niamh called her name as Cliona darted for the front door, halting with her hand on the door handle when she heard Danika say her name this time. Closing her eyes for a second to try and calm the rapid beating of her heart, Cliona turned round and faced Danika.

Danika's expression was blank, but her eyes, those piercing blue eyes held a mixture of emotions that Cliona couldn't unpack while trying to make sense of her own. Folding her arms across her chest, the hem of her shirt rose to expose more of her skin, and Cliona had to snap her gaze back up when she realized that she had been staring at the creamy colour of Danika's skin.

"You were really gonna cut and run, weren't you?"

Cliona swallowed hard, unable to lie to Danika and tell her that she wasn't planning on it, but here Cliona was standing at the door, ready to run. A muscle ticked in Danika's jaw.

"I guess that answers the question for me. After last night, I thought that you'd be over whatever it is that's keeping you from giving us a shot, but I can see that you've already made up your mind."

"Danika..." Cliona began to say, but Danika was already shaking her head.

"It's grand. I get it. I'm good enough to fuck but not to keep around. Got it. Loud and clear. Hey, it's grand. We had fun and now it doesn't have to be awkward or anything. I absolve you of any regret and shame for sleeping with me. See ya around, Cliona."

Before Cliona could respond to Danika's proclamation, the other woman was gone. Cliona let her head fall back with a thud against the door, and she let go of a shuddering breath. There was a large part of her that demanded that she march right on up to Danika's room and make her see that the reason why she was freaking out was because she had fallen in love with Danika...maybe she always had been.

The people she loved had the power to destroy her, just like her parents had once almost destroyed her. She had clawed her way back from that heartbreak, though it had taken years, and Cliona wasn't sure she was strong enough to do it again if Danika decided to break her heart.

"Are you okay?"

Cliona looked over to see Oli watching her. It was obvious that he and Niamh had heard what Danika had said, and that Cliona deserved the disappointment in Oli's eyes. Tears threatened to spill out of her own eyes as she managed to grind out one simple word. "No."

"I'm not going to interfere. This is yours and Dani's business. But I was once standing where Dani was, as a person who didn't feel like they were worthy of the love they wanted from someone. We might be rockstars who ooze confidence and attitude on stage, but we are human beings too, who just want to be loved for who we are. Danika sounds like she could do that for you...but can you love her like she deserves to be loved? I think that's what you need to ask yourself."

Oli inclined his head as he went back into his house and his words bounced around in her head long after she'd slipped out the door, and gone home, her own bed feeling cold and lonely after last night. Cliona wanted to be brave, to have the courage to admit to herself, and to Danika what it was that she wanted, what she craved so much. There was a fine line between protecting her heart and self-sabotage, as Cliona felt like she skirted the line between one and the other...

CHAPTER TWENTY-FOUR

Danika

DANIKA KNEW full well that Oli was trying to distract her from what had happened with Cliona by getting all excited about directing the music video for the song she and Heartache Melody hadn't even recorded yet. That was why Oli had invited the entire band over to run through ideas, as he didn't want to leave Niamh on her own.

The band turned up, and it wasn't long before Niamh had kissed Oli on the cheek and said that she was going for a lie-down. Oli looked worried, but the moment everyone started to get down to talking about the video, Oli focused.

Jameson played the recording he had on his phone of the song, as Oli closed his eyes and soaked in the song. Luna was grinning, her fingers drumming out a beat on her leg as it played. The song ended, and Oli told Jameson to play it again.

Declan smiled as Jameson hit play again, knowing Oli was in the zone. Rhys went and brought them back drinks from the fridge, the poor man blushing when Danika winked at him, making Luna burst out laughing, Danika joining her when Olin shushed them both.

Oli opened his eyes with a smirk. "I think I have it."

Then Oli explained to them the vision of what the music video could be. He wanted Danika and Jameson walking around a house like it had been theirs, with Luna in one room, Rhys in another, and then Declan. They would sing as they walked through the house, missing each other, so like, when Danika walked into a room, Jameson would just have left.

"We'll have it grey and dark and then have flashes of memories of Danika and Jameson as a happy couple. Have those in colour. It will be brilliant."

Danika glanced over at Jameson, who shifted uncomfortably in his seat, rubbing the back of his neck. "I dunno, Oli."

"Jameson, it will be like a mini-movie. Showing how love can turn to ashes. You guys like it right?"

The rest of the band nodded, so Oli looked expectantly at Jameson. Danika was worried that he didn't like the idea of being the main focus of the music video, but the moment Jameson said the next words,

Danika understood what was stopping Jameson from committing to the video.

"I'll need to run it by Sinéad."

Oli looked like he was about to argue, as Jameson got to his feet and went out into the back garden, Declan catching Danika's eye before he went out after Jameson. Oli was still oblivious to it all, grumbling to himself until Danika smacked him on the knee and he turned to glare at her.

"For a smart man, you can be a dumbass sometimes." When Oli still looked like he had no clue what Danika was trying to say, she continued. "How do you think Niamh would feel for your next video if you were getting up close and personal with some dancer or video bunny?"

"Why would I have a video bunny in my video? Have you seen my music videos?"

Christ on a fucking bike...Oli was making this waaay harder than it had to be.

"Not the goddamn point. Okay, listen as I say this. Do you not think that Cathal, Shay, and even Andi would not feel uncomfortable if their partner was pretending to be all loved up with some girl in a music video without being consulted? Even if that girl is a lesbian who has no interest in Jameson's cock."

Poor Rhys, who had been halfway through taking a drink of his Coke, spat it out with a choked sound as Luna cackled with laughter, though her explanation seemed to get through to Oli in his creative haze. Rhys shook his head as he got up to get something to clean up his mess, but Luna was still crying with laughter as the boys came back in.

Declan glanced at Luna, then cocked a brow. "What we miss?"

Danika flashed a grin full of teeth. "Nothing much. Just me explaining to Oli that Jameson needed to loop Sinéad in on his idea to make sure she was comfortable with me and Jay playing pretend, even if Sinéad knows I have no interest in Jameson's cock...or any cock mind. And Rhys made a mess."

Declan barked out a laugh as Jameson shook his head, then sighed, looking at Oli. "The video idea is right, but Danika's right. I need to run it by Sinéad and if she's not okay, we go back to the beginning...or cut the romantic bits."

Oli nodded, and they changed the conversation to other things and time seemed to slip by as Jameson asked if he should ring for food. Danika laughed as Niamh appeared in the kitchen, yawning.

"Did someone mention food? I'm starving."

Jameson took everyone's order, then called it in as Danika watched Niamh and Oli share a look, then Oli ducked out of the room and came back with two boxes. Niamh took one from Oli, then handed it to Jameson when he came back in, telling him not to open it just yet.

Oli came over and sat on the arm of the chair beside her, then handed Danika the other box. When they got the nod from the couple to open the boxes, Jameson quickly took the lid off the box, and then he was hugging his sister as she cried, and no one knew what the hell was going on.

Danika was slightly afraid to open hers.

When Oli nudged her with his shoulder, Danika carefully slipped off the lid of the box and stared at the contents. It was a small Babygro, with the words, "I can't wait to meet my godmother," on it and Danika snapped her gaze to Oli's. "Me? Really?"

"Who else would I have?" Oli said, very amused by Danika's question.

"Um...JJ?"

Oli barked out a laugh. "I'm sure JJ would have been delighted to have been asked to be godmother, but Dani, I couldn't have asked for a better aunt for my kid. Or a better sister."

Danika felt wetness on her face, and she realized that she was crying. "Fucking hell, Oli. You made me leak. Don't tell anyone."

Then before Oli could say anything, Danika lunged for him throwing her arms around his neck and hugging him hard. The rest of the band cheered and offered congratulations, then Danika leaned back and held Oli's gaze. "If the priest asks me do I renounce Satan, what the hell am I supposed to say?"

"You lie your ass off like I intend to do," Oli said after he barked out a laugh.

Danika detangled herself from Oli to go and hung

Niamh, who was swiping tears from her eyes. "Thank you. This means more than you know."

Niamh gave her a wicked smile. "This means you need to stick around now. Oli told me there is a house down the road for sale. It would be nice to have two babysitters living so nearby."

Danika gave Niamh an unamused look, then she looked over at Oli, who shrugged. "I have the details in my office. I told my estate agent to hold off on any offers until you've had a look. If you don't want a house, there's a loft available down the road from Rebel Books."

"You have it all planned out, don't you?"

Oli merely shrugged, as Danika glanced over at the band, and Declan mimicked Oli with a shrug. "There are a dozen flights to London every day from Cork. You'd commute faster than if you lived in London. Besides, my studio is always open to you, I'll even give ya a key."

"Besides," Luna interjected with a grin, "If you stay, I'll get Cathal to fit you in for a tattoo."

Oli looked shocked by Luna's declaration, as everyone laughed. This was what Danika had been missing in her life. A tribe, a family, and even though she decided to let them think that she hadn't already decided to stay before this afternoon, Danika knew that she had found her place in the world.

However, the last piece was still evading her...

Pushing thoughts of Cliona out of her head,

Danika let loose an exaggerated sigh. "Okay, show me the goddam brochures of the gaffs. But just so you know, it was Luna pimping out her boyfriend that won me over."

The food arrived then, as did Luna's pimped-out boyfriend, who seemed mildly amused and perplexed to have rockstars arguing over his tattoo skills. Danika went to the fridge to get herself a drink, Oli coming to stand beside her.

"I'm glad you're staying," Oli told her quietly. "You were the one thing I missed. And JJ, but he might be here next summer, so we just need to persuade him to get a house here then."

Danika grinned at Oli. "Me too. And we can convince JJ. We always do."

CHAPTER TWENTY-FIVE

Cliona

CLIONA HAD BEEN ready to turn Niamh's invite to come over for lunch down, however when her friend told her that she would be alone all afternoon and that Oli wouldn't feel so bad about having to go to London at short notice, Cliona knew she couldn't refuse.

She'd been itching to ask where Danika was, but Cliona reigned in the urge. Danika hadn't texted her since the morning after the night they spent together. Not that she blamed Danika after how stupid she had acted, but still.

Niamh's mam was leaving as Cliona drove into the driveway, and they stopped to share a few words before Cliona knocked on the front door, and then headed inside. Cliona walked into the kitchen to the most amazing smell, and almost groaned when she saw the stack of chocolate brownies on the counter.

Her friend was sat in one of the armchairs, a fluffy blanket over her legs as she smiled at Cliona, and motioned for her to sit. Niamh's hair was pulled back into a ponytail, and even though she had no makeup, Niamh looked radiant.

"Oh thank god you are here. Lemmie just text Oli and tell him that you're here so he can stop bugging me every thirty seconds. He's driving me crazy. I love him, but if he hadn't of had to go to London today with Andi and Danika, I might have killed him."

Cliona chuckled as she sat down across from Niamh, holding up the bag she had brought. "Well, I brought you that new crime author that you liked. And a few other books to keep you occupied."

Niamh's eyes sparkled. "You are awesome. And before you ask, no, I did not make the brownies. Mam did. Make us a cuppa and grab some because if I get up, mini Scott might just decide to wake up and kick me like they did last night at three AM."

Cliona got up, made some tea, and grabbed some brownies before retaking her seat. They chatted about Rebel Books, about Nessa finally having a move-in date to the apartment above the bookstore, and about how Cliona's new display that was blowing it up on social media. She could tell that Niamh wanted to talk about something else, and from the tension in the pregnant woman's body, Cliona didn't want her to feel stressed out because of whatever it was she needed to bring up.

"Come on, Niamh. Just spit it out. You'll feel better."

Niamh balanced her mug on her knee, a faint blush on her cheeks. "I'm mortified about the other morning."

"I know. I behaved badly with Danika and I'm sorry about you and Oli having to see that."

Niamh looked momentarily surprised, chewed on her bottom lip, and then said. "No, Cliona. I meant that I was dying of embarrassment that you walked in on me and Oli in the kitchen."

Cliona's lips formed an 'O'. It wasn't that she had forgotten the completely insane and embarrassing situation, but her own stupid behaviour had distracted her from thinking too hard about it. Niamh obviously thought that Cliona had been dodging her calls and texts because of that. Cliona didn't want Niamh to feel bad about it.

In a few years, they'd probably all laugh about it.

"Yano, I hadn't even thought about it... until now."

Niamh covered her face in her hands. "Oh my god! I'm bringing up something you didn't even register enough to think about."

Cliona curst out laughing and Nimah, whose face was red when she removed her hands, laughed too.

With a grin on her face, Cliona leaned back in her chair. "I totally get it. Oli's very *attentive*."

Niamh cast her a look saying she had caught Cliona's meaning. "Oli has spent his nights when I'm asleep reading online medical studies. That morning, he was telling me that this article he read, said that in the months prior to labour, vaginal stimulation and sex could help ease labour. He was trying to test a theory."

Biting the inside of her mouth to stop herself from laughing, Cliona didn't hear a complaint in Nimah's tone. "That must be very hard to have your hot boyfriend want to help ease your labour by having sexy time with you."

Rolling her eyes, Niamh then pinned Cliona with a stare. "I'll talk about sex with my hot rockstar if you are ready to talk about sex with yours."

Cliona made a point of drinking the remnants of her tea, before setting the mug down on the coffee table. "The sex isn't the problem, Niamh. It was..."

"Life changing," Niamh said softly, a smile curving her lips.

"Ya. I think before, I still had my parent's voices in my head to tell me that touching a woman like that was sinful. But with Danika, there were no voices. It felt right."

Niamh drained her own mug and then set it down. "Then why?"

Cliona knew what Niamh was asking, and to be

honest, it felt good to talk to someone who was once in the same position as she was now. However, Oli and Danika were completely different people. Or were they?

"I dunno," Cliona admitted, twirling the ends of her hair between her fingers. "I'm proud to be who I am. But I dunno if I'm ready for all the exposure that comes with being Danika Keane's latest arm candy. And I know that you had that with Oli, but Niamh, you are gorgeous."

"Cliona do not make me yell at you because you think that you aren't good enough to stand beside Danika. And I've had minimal exposure...though Oli thinks it's 'cause the fans are respectful of the fact I'm pregnant. Yes, at first, the constant asking for selfies and autographs was...disconcerting, but that's who Oli is. I love that he is so fan-focused. Danika is too. I don't know her as well as I do Oli, but Danika is family now. I want the best for you both."

Cliona sighed. "If I'm being honest, I want to try with her. I just think we need to reset and start fresh. When we were chatting online, and no one knew, it was exciting and I could be myself because Dani, Danika, accepted all of me, and even sympathized over my parents. It's one thing to go from online dating, to really dating, especially when she is who she is...there's no anonymity when your partner is one of the world's most lusted after lesbians."

"Well, considering I'm having a baby with a man

who was once called every housewife's fantasy, I feel like I'm uniquely qualified to tell you that people will still lust after them. Hell, I know for a fact that Jameson and the rest of the band were in some hottest 30 under 30 thing in some Irish mag. My mam put Jamie's picture on the fridge."

They both laughed, knowing Jameson was not all that comfortable with the limelight.

"But, I had it easy," Niamh admitted, shifting in her chair. "Others haven't. So, there is both bad and good. Shay had some hassle after her and Rhys went public. Nothing that badass couldn't handle, but enough that Rhys posted about it on social media. In the end, Cliona, none of that matters. What you have to decide is, are your feelings for Danika stronger than the fear instilled in you by your parents? And if you pass on the chance to be happy with Danika, then are they winning?"

Cliona knew that Niamh was right. Things finally started to make sense. Cliona hadn't realized just how much her parents had and were still influencing her. That needed to stop. She had to start fighting for what she wanted, not settling for lonely days at home with no one to share life with. There were people out there who didn't have people like Niamh to call their friend.

"You know Danika's staying, right?"

Cliona was dragged from her thoughts as she looked at Niamh. "She is?"

Niamh gave a slight nod of her head. "Yup. She's

going to check on a few places nearby and she if anything clicks. Her and Oli are in London for a meeting and to get some of her stuff. I think Danika was lonely in London without Oli and JJ. And her and Jameson have become solid friends."

The thought of having Danika in Cork as her base sent a little thrill along Cliona's spine. Things might not work out between them, but Cliona would rather regret that she tried and failed, instead of regretting that she never gave Danika a fair shot. All the rest, they could sort that out when and if a problem arose.

Cliona was done living half a life.

"Have you never wanted to see the world?"

That was the question that had been plaguing her since Danika had uttered it, and now? Now, Cliona realized that she just hadn't wanted to see the world alone. But she would very much like to see it with Danika, if she could convince her rockstar that she was all in with her.

Chapter Twenty-Six

Danika

DANIKA HAD BEEN SO eager to leave London, that it made her wonder how she ever considered it her home. Her apartment was a showhouse, and that was because Danika hadn't changed much from when she signed the lease, even though the contract allowed it. Danika had always assumed she'd move, but in the end, it was a place where she came to shut out the world.

They'd gone for dinner, her, Oli, and Andi, the night before returning to Cork, and had been surprised at the restaurant by JJ, who just rocked up without telling anyone. They also got to celebrate JJ landing the role he was dying to get, playing a detective in Cork for a new crime show. It had been signed up for multiple seasons, so that meant once everything was settled, he'd be in Cork too.

Apparently, he'd already started looking at houses.

Danika was happy...but Cliona was never far from her mind.

When they'd all gone back to hers, Oli going to give Niamh a call, and Andi had a late night/early morning call with Charlie, Danika had found herself alone with JJ. They were sat out on her balcony, looking over London, drinking some expensive chardonnay JJ had brought with him. Danika had been gazing out over the city, drinking in the lights for one of the last times probably, when she felt JJ looking at her.

"What?"

JJ just smiled, and took a sip of his fancy drink, and it reminded her of when they had been at his country estate, and Danika had been staring at him.

"You look happy, darling."

"Is that your way of saying I look like a miserable bitch most of the time?"

JJ chortled, rolling his eyes. "Well, you do get paid a lot of money to play the miserable bitch. But no. You seem relaxed."

"Are you telling me I'm uptight?"

"Jesus fucking Christ, Dani...take the compliment," JJ said with an exasperated sound and Danika kept her lips firmly shut.

"Oli said that you've settled into Irish life easily. And before you come back and ask me if me and Oli have been talking about you, of course we have."

That made Danika roll her eyes, but the love in her heart that she had for JJ and Oli, and the love they had for her was so obvious, that she couldn't chastise them for whatever had them discussing her.

"Does it have anything to do with the manager of Niamh's bookshop?"

Danika shrugged, reaching for the bottle, and filling her glass, taking a large gulp before she replied to JJ. "I don't know. Without you and Oli here, life got so mundane. I think that's why I slept with Lola. I was lonely and drunk. But there is always something going on in Cork."

JJ leaned forward, setting his glass down on the metal table in front of him. "Dani, darling. You could have called us. We never would have wanted you to feel alone."

Danika smiled over at JJ. "I know. And maybe that's why I didn't call. You two would have dropped everything to come to me. Oli would have left Niamh, and you would have flown thousands of miles, all because I was feeling a little sorry for myself."

"Would you or Oli not do the same if it was me? I believe you both have done so, making sure that you both had shows at the same time in the place I was filming."

"We're family. We show up." Danika told him.

"Exactly," JJ confirmed before he reached over and took her hand in his. "Go and find your happiness, Danika. If this woman is who you want, tell her. You have the luxury of being able to show the world the

person you love. Do not waste that because you're afraid."

"JJ..." Danika said, her heart aching for her brother.

But JJ flashed her his movie star smile, the one that both Danika and Oli knew was fake. "Nope, no melancholy tonight. I made my choice all those years ago and for my career, it was the best path for me."

Danika and Oli had been there for JJ when he'd had his heart broken, and the mystery man that JJ had never gotten over was out there somewhere. Danika wished that the world wasn't so fucked up that JJ feared he would be typecast because of his sexuality. She wanted him to be happy.

Her decision to confess her feelings to Cliona had been made before her trip to London, but after JJ's little sort of motivational speech, Danika was more determined than ever. It had taken a lot of convincing for Niamh to give Danika Cliona's home address, but when Danika told Niamh that she was going to try and convince Cliona to give them a shot, and she didn't want to embarrass Cliona by making her declaration in Rebel Books, Niamh gave her the address.

Oli had fist-bumped her as she went out, got into her new car, a sleek black Audi with tinted windows, and drove through the rain to the address Niamh had given her. The house was nestled in a housing estate with a dozen other houses and Danika wondered if she could live in a place like this.

Her security would have an aneurysm at all the entry points.

That is once they realized she had dodged them again.

Pulling the car up to the front of the house, Danika gave herself a little pep talk before she got out, ran up the steps to the house, and knocked on the door. Rain pelted down on her, cold as it landed on her skin, but Danika was fired up on the inside and she just had to get everything off her chest.

A little bit of rain never killed anyone, right?

The front door opened to reveal Cliona, her eyes widening when she saw it was Danika on the other side of the door. "Danika? When did you get back?"

Hoped surged inside Danika's chest that Cliona knew that she hadn't been in Ireland.

"Yesterday. I picked up my car this morning so then I came here."

"Okay. Would you like to come in?"

Danika nodded as Cliona stepped away to let her enter. Closing the door behind her, Danika leaned against the door for support. Cliona was wearing jeans and a tee but she looked beautiful. Danika wanted to kiss her, to use her body to convince Cliona just how fucking good they could be together. But she needed to use her words.

"I'm staying in Cork," Danika told her, but from Cliona's expression, the object of her desire already knew that. "I'm trying to convince Oli to start up our own record label, but that's not the point. Fuck, I'm already messing this up and I haven't even begun."

Danika inhaled a breath, not giving Cliona a chance to say anything as she just rambled on. "I've made a lot of mistakes. I fucked up a lot. I'm cynical and foul-mouthed and sometimes, I react before my brain can tell me it's a bad idea. But with you, I don't feel like I have all of these bad qualities.

I want to give us a shot. If that means keeping it on the down-low for now, I'm good with that. But I'd be lying if I didn't admit that I wanted to walk down the street holding your hand. That I wanted to kiss you in crowded places and not give a fuck who sees us. I'm here now, cutting myself open for the first time in my life and asking you to take a chance on me. To take a chance on us."

Cliona just stood there staring at Danika, and Danika suddenly felt like she had made a massive mistake. She had put all her cards on the table and Cliona was just standing there looking at her like Danika had lost her mind.

Fuck, this was what it felt like to have your heart break...

Danika closed her eyes, and leaned her head against the door, her heart pounding in her chest. When she felt the ghost of a touch on her cheek, Danika's eyes sprang open. Cliona was in front of her, a hand on her cheek. "I want to give us a shot too."

Grabbing Cliona's face in her hands, Danika kissed

the hell out of her, and by the end of the licking, the tasting, the touching, they were both breathless.

"So what now?" Danika asked, delighted at the mischievous smile that curled Cliona's lips.

Cliona popped the button of Danika's jeans and began to push them down over Danika's hips, her fingers grazing her flesh and Danika sucked in a breath. "I think it would be a great idea to get you out of those wet clothes."

Danika kicked off her shoes, then her jeans, and stood in the hallway of Cliona's house, as the other woman kissed her hard once, then her thumbs teased the sides of her lace panties, then they too were gone and Cliona lowered herself to her knees, and Danika was a slave to her touch.

CHAPTER TWENTY-SEVEN

Danika

AFTER SPENDING a lot of time over the last few days making up for lost time, Danika had decided that if she wanted to firmly plant roots in Cork, and show Cliona that she was serious about them, then Danika needed to pry herself from being in bed with Cliona and go and talk to Oli.

Though it had been Cliona who had to be the one to get out of bed first this morning, her shift at Rebel Books limiting the time they had for some very sexy shower time. Danika had been waiting for the novelty of the sex with Cliona to wear off like it had with other partners, but this time, every time they made love, every touch, every kiss; it all felt different...good different...like Danika knew she would never tire of the way Cliona touched her.

She was still grinning like an idiot when she walked into Oli's music room a couple of hours later. In true Oli style, he was sat behind the piano, dressed in just a pair of shorts and his array of tattoos. Danika nudged him with her shoulder, and he rolled his eyes, before sliding over so she could sit beside him.

Oli started to play some keys, and Danika joined in, and they just played together for the longest time, the sound so fucking beautiful it had lured Niamh from wherever she'd been to linger in the doorway, her eyes closed and the biggest smile on her face.

When they finished, Danika leaned her head against Oli's shoulder. "Man, I've missed just doing shit like this with you. Maybe we do need to commit to working on a song together."

Oli replied in a very deadpan tone. "I've heard Calvin would be open to having us both on his new Ibiza party song."

Danika barked out a laugh, shaking her head. "Never gonna happen."

Danika got up off the bench, as Niamh came over and wrapped her arms around Oli. She lifted on hand up to play with the now longer strands of Oli's hair, and Oli closed his eyes. She had never seen him look so at ease.

"We haven't seen you in the last few days," Niamh mentioned tentatively.

Danika grinned, showing Niamh all her pearly whites. "I've been having very dirty and satisfying sex with your shop manager. She is very committed...to her job. Not even my hot body could make her call in sick so we could test the suspension in my car."

Oli chuckled as Niamh flushed pink in her cheeks and that made Danika laugh. "Oli, if Niamh is blushing at my dirty mouth, then you mustn't be talking to her in the right way when you guys are naked."

Oli opened his mouth to retort, but Niamh clamped a hand over his mouth, and then let out a squeak. "Oh my god, Oli."

"I told you I don't go around licking woman I'm not interested in."

"Well, I'm the only woman you need to be thinking about licking. Oh for fuck sake, you two are rubbing off on me, I'm starting to lose my filter." Niamh groaned but Oli and Danika were just laughing so hard that Niamh grumbled and said she was going to get a start on dinner.

"I'll text Cliona and tell her to come here once her shift is done. I need backup against you two."

That had made them laugh even harder, until Danika's chest ached, and tears came out of her eyes. When they had finally gotten themselves together, Danika flopped down on the sofa by the wall, let her feet rest on the arm of the chair, and then huffed out a breath.

"Dani."

She put her arm over her eyes. "I told Bruno I was

done with the label. He called me a dried-up hasbeen who was hanging on your success and without the creative team behind me, I would be a flop. He told me that goth rock was dead, and I was too old now to be singing about how much I like pussy, or how much of a bitch I am."

"I never liked Bruno," Oli mumbled, tinkering with the keys of the piano again. "He has the personality of a house plant. And a plastic one at that."

Danika snorted, trying to see if this was the moment she should try and persuade Oli, but her friend asked her a question then, giving her the perfect opening. "What are you gonna do now Dani?"

"Well, right now, I'm going to try and talk my best friend into investing in starting our own indie label, like we always dreamed of doing."

"Dani..." Oli began, his fingers faltering over the keys.

She sat up straight as Oli turned to look at her. "Hear me out before you say no. With how good you are with the money side of things, and the fact that the two of us would be in charge, we could make it work. Hell, ask the Heartache Melody lads to invest so it's a big ole family affair. When we were growing up, we had all these plans. Think about it, Oli. No one to tell us what music we should or should not be releasing. No one asking us to be anyone but who we are as artists"

Danika could tell by the spark in Oli's eyes that his

interest was piqued. Sometimes, you needed to leave Oli think about something and look at all the outcomes before he came to a conclusion.

"You can set your own schedule. When mini Scott is old enough to be going to school, tour in the summer holidays and take them with us. Do like Korn did and have a family values type tour and you, me, and the Heartache Melody lads can all hit the road together."

Danika was excited at the prospect of it all. She could hear it in her voice, and wanted Oli to be just as excited as she was. "We could give artists that didn't have the opportunities like we did a shot. Nurture them so that no one ends up like you when you might have lost your voice. It wouldn't just be a business; it would be a family."

Oli rested his chin on his fist as he leaned forward. Danika knew him well enough to know that the cogs in his brain were turning round and round in his head, while he worked shit out. Danika was already smiling, knowing that the idea of using the business to create a family was always something Oli wanted.

"I guess you already have a name picked out in all for this hypothetical business?"

Danika smirked, feeling like she had already won this battle. "Well, how do you feel about Rebel Records?" Oli quirked a brow and Danika shrugged. "I mean, every other goddamn business in Cork seems to be named Rebel something. We've got Rebel Racers,

Rebel PR, Rebel Ink, Rebel Books...why not Rebel Records? Not sure what Declan and Noah are gonna call their gym but I'm sure Rebel will be in it. Would be rude to break with what seems to be a fucking tradition, right?"

Oli huffed out a laugh, and ran a hand through his hair. "Danika, I'm not saying yes, yet...but you've made some good points. I was stressing about touring when the baby got older. And that idea about having us do our own tour is kinda genius."

Danika punched the air and lifted her legs up and down as Oli rolled his eyes. "Baby steps, Dani. We need to sit down and get a plan on paper, look at financials and legalities, and all the fun stuff that comes with being your own boss. If...if it all pans out and looks like a good investment, then I'm in."

With a surge, Danika launched off the chair and was hugging Oli tightly as he sighed that sigh of his, that Danika knew so well, that he was already on board, and they were finally going to make the dream they had thought of in their dorm in boarding school.

Letting Oli go, Danika decided to let Oli in on a little secret that she had kept from him for a little while. "Emerald Records is hemorrhaging money and not even the prospect of Heartache Melody's success can save them. They have no money to send the band on tour. We should swoop in and buy their contract."

"How the hell did you find out about that?"

Danika grinned. "One of the boards' daughters is a

fan. I did one of those happy birthday things for her and her mam slipped me the info. She said they might go bust by the end of the year. Something about a fraud charge."

Oli rose off the bench. "I need to talk to Dec and Andi; this is big for them. For the band."

"We both have the funds to help them out. It's what family does."

They were grinning as they went downstairs where Niamh had finished making dinner, and Cliona was sat at the counter, her smile warming Danika as she walked over and kissed Cliona, and it felt like everything had finally started to feel like home.

CHAPTER TWENTY-EIGHT

Cliona

CLIONA HAD BEEN SURPRISED at how easy it had
been to slip into being with Danika. To be honest,
Cliona was ashamed to admit that she was worried that
Danika would want to party every night, but the rockstar was happy to curl up on the couch or in bed and
binge a show. On the one night where they had been
supposed to head out with the Heartache Melody
crew, Danika had asked Cliona if she minded if they
just stayed in, and had been asleep an hour later.

After lots and lots of really great sex, they had
finally taken the time to define where they were headed
with their relationship. Danika had asked her how she
felt about making it social media official, and Cliona
had been honest that she wasn't ready for that just yet.
Then Danika had countered, asking if it was okay for

her to change her status to in a relationship, because none of her previous lovers who were blowing up her phone believed her.

Cliona had felt a surge of jealousy, and accepted that emotion though, but forced herself not to check any of Danika's socials in case Danika was getting grief over it all. Danika was also adamant that they were each other's girlfriends. When Cliona said that they didn't need any labels, Danika had said that she wanted people to know that Danika was Cliona's. It had seemed so important to Danika that Cliona couldn't argue with her, plus she liked being Danika Keane's girlfriend.

Danika had told Cliona that she didn't want them to hide away either. And they hadn't. last night they had gone for dinner with Niamh and Oli, and after spending the day looking at places Danika was interested in buying, they had stopped at a pub to grab some early dinner before heading back to Oli's for a movie night.

Tonight, the other couple were at Niamh's parents and would be home by the time Danika and Cliona arrived back at Oli's from a date night. They had a nice meal out, with a few interruptions. Danika had looked at Cliona as if she was trying to gauge her reaction when a fan asked for a picture, but Cliona had just asked the young woman if she wanted Cliona to take the picture, and Danika had given her this massive smile.

It was strange to see Danika in her element, chatting to fans, but in a good way. This was part of the industry that Danika loved, and that was why her fans loved her. It was one of the reasons why Cliona loved her.

Not that Cliona had been brave enough just yet to tell Danika that. Everything was so new and great; she didn't want to ruin it by putting pressure on Danika to say it back. They had plenty of time for that.

They finished their meal, then Danika went to the bar and gave the staff a very generous tip, before telling the bar the next round was on her. The pub erupted with a cheer as Danika slipped her hand into Cliona's and they walked out.

"You know, that was nice of you to do what you did," Cliona told her, giving Danika a quick press on the cheek.

Danika shrugged, like her actions were nothing. "The manager came over and was all apologies when we kept getting interrupted. I told her that I was skilled at eating a lot in a short space of time. That it was all part of the job, so not to worry. I think she was worried that I'd post some shit about being harassed. I don't think they know what harassment looks like, but that wasn't it."

They walked in silence to where Danika had parked her car, and Danika stopped to draw Cliona in for a kiss, her hands on Cliona's hips, Cliona's arms around Danika's neck.

"Yano, we could blow Oli and Niamh off and just go back to yours."

The heat in Danika's eyes made Cliona want to do the same, but she laughed and stepped out of Danika's embrace, laughing harder when Danika glared at her.

"While that sounds epic, we made a promise. And I do not want to have Oli rock up to Rebel Books and announce to the whole store that we blew him off to go have sex again."

Cliona wasn't even exaggerating when she said that Oli had done just that. Thankfully, it had been at a lull time, and not too many customers had been in the shop. Sorcha had found it hilarious though, and teased Cliona about it all week.

Danika wiggled her brows. "It's not like he was lying. We did blow them off last week to go have sex. It was your idea too."

"You're incorrigible," Cliona told her girlfriend.

"It's one of the reasons why you keep me around."

Cliona leaned forward to give Danika a quick peck on the lips, then turned round to head to the car and froze. Her mother was standing on the other side of the street with one of her church friends, looking at her with such disapproval that it made her stomach sink.

She must have squeezed Danika's hand a little too hard, because the other woman looked at her, then tracked where her eyes were focused on, and then she asked Cliona if she was okay.

"That's my mam." Cliona managed to grind out, unsure of what to do as her mother walked toward her, and Cliona thought she was gonna walk on by her again and ignore her.

"We can just walk on past her as if we don't see her. If that's what you want."

Cliona was about to nod at Danika, but the woman with her mother seemed to recognise her then, looked at her friend, and frowned. This was going to be awful.

"Cliona McCarthy is that you?" The woman asked as she walked right over to Cliona and then gave her a hug. "I haven't seen you in donkeys years, girl."

"Hey, Mrs. Lyons. How is Bert? And the boys?"

Mrs Lyons snorted. "Still giving me grey hairs. But they are happy and that's what's important. Gary has two kids with his wife. And Sean, he and his husband got married last year."

That surprised Cliona to see Mrs Lyons talking so openly about her son being gay, and Cliona couldn't help but glance at her mother, who was scowling at Mrs Lyons.

"Cliona, who is this?"

Cliona was still kinda shook, so it was up to Danika to take the lead. "Hey, it's nice to meet you. I'm Danika, Cliona's girlfriend."

Her mother flinched at the word, and Danika caught it, and Cliona could see her hold back her temper. Mrs Lyons was staring at Danika, like she

SUSAN HARRIS

recognised her but Danika's music wasn't the kind of music they played at church bake sales.

"Do I know you? you look very familiar?"

Danika grinned, and gave a nonchalant shrug of her shoulders. "I sing a little."

"Danika's being modest," Cliona heard herself say, heard the pride in her tone. "She is a very famous rock-star who has used her music to speak out for those of us in our community who feel like they aren't accepted."

"Danika? As in Danika Keane. My Sean is a big fan. He and his husband had your song Late Night Lover as their first dance. Not my cup of tea but it fits them."

Danika grinned, the delight making her blue eyes shimmer in the faint streetlight. "That's awesome. I'll sign some stuff and leave them with Cliona at Rebel Books. Pop in next week and you can send them to your son."

They said their goodbyes then, and her mother hadn't uttered a syllable to her, and that made Cliona feel so sad. Danika lifted her hand and kissed her knuckles before Cliona heard her call out.

"Mrs McCarthy?"

Her mother turned and looked at Danika, who said. "Your daughter is kind, and caring, and the most amazing woman I know. It's your loss that you can't accept her. She hasn't murdered someone; Cliona just happens to like women. There are much worse people out there, even in religious circles."

Cliona loved that Danika was standing up for her when she didn't feel ready to stand up for herself.

Her mother ran her gaze over Danika. "I bet your parents are disappointed with the life choices you have made."

Danika barked out a laugh. "My father was nothing but a sperm donor and my mother is on a cruise fucking men young enough to be her son. I think my life choices are my own. Are you happy with your life choices?"

Danika pulled her away then, as Cliona heard Mrs Lyons busting a gut with laughter. When they were in the car, Danika refused to let go of her hand as she said. "I'm sorry if I overstepped, but I hated seeing you frightened of that crusty old bat. And I love you too much to just stand there and do nothing."

Cliona's heart raced, as Danika glanced at her with cautious eyes and Cliona reached over to caress her face. "I love you, too. Thank you for looking out for me."

They smiled, and kissed until the windows were fogged up...and they ended up being late for movie night...not that either of them cared.

CHAPTER TWENTY-NINE

Danika

THINGS HAD BEEN MOVING RAPIDLY since Danika had started to immerse herself into life in Cork. Oli and her had been working on the plans for Rebel Records, with Declan and the band on board for them to acquire Heartache Melody's contract now that Emerald Records was officially going bust. The first thing Oli did was sign up Rebel PR to handle everything with the label.

Yesterday, Danika had gone with Oli to look at one of the last remaining warehouses across from where Andi and Declan had their home, where Rebel PR would be based, and where the gym was. Danika had joked that they should rename the business park to Rebel Avenue, making everyone laugh when she started to sing, we gonna rock down to Rebel Avenue.

The following day, Rhys had put up a sign at the entrance with the name Rebel Avenue on it.

Oli had put a bid in late last night, and this morning, they'd signed on the dotted line, and now were proud owners of a warehouse that would be turned into a recording studio. It had been Oli's idea to make the upstairs into little living spaces, so that new artists could have somewhere to stay if they had nowhere else to go.

Buying the warehouse had barely put a dent in her finances, and while all of the places Oli's estate agent had shown her were amazing, none of them felt quite right. When she mentioned it to Oli and Niamh, Oli had given her a bemused smile, then proceeded to tell Danika what was wrong with all the places.

"They don't feel like a place you want to call home because it doesn't feel right without Cliona."

When Danika had narrowed her gaze, Oli laughed. "It's true. When I was looking at all the stupid houses the estate agent was showing me with gold baths and infinity pool – I mean, who in their right mind needs an infinity pool in Ireland – I knew they weren't quite right. Even then I was looking at a home for me and Niamh, even if she wasn't that keen on me back then."

Rolling her eyes, Niamh smacked Oli on the shoulder. "Get to the point, Oli."

"My point is," Oli said as he took Niamh's hand in his. "I would never have been happy rattling round in a house like this without Niamh. We didn't have a stable homelife as kids, Dani. We only ever wanted to be rich and famous enough to put down roots and even when we had the money, we couldn't do it. We just needed the right women to make us want to stay in one place."

Niamh leaned into Oli, her hand on her bump. "Smooth talker."

Danika had understood then exactly what Oli was saying to her. She wanted a home with Cliona. She wanted someone to come home to, to stay up late watching stupid reality TV. She wanted family dinners, and people walking in and out of her home like they had keys.

Danika was still thinking it over when she went back to Cliona's house later that night, and picked at her Chinese food. She was so lost in her own head, that she didn't hear Cliona say her name until she reached out and touched her hand.

With a jerk, Danika blinked and looked at Cliona, who looked concerned.

"Hey, you were miles away? Everything okay?"

Play it cool...play it cool...

"How attached are you to this house?" Danika blurted out and Cliona dropped her fork. Shit, she was going about this the wrong way, but Danika didn't know how to be subtle.

"Dani, what's going on?" Cliona asked, a slight tremor in her voice, and Danika thought that Cliona might be worried that the shiny had worn off and Danika was trying to cut and run.

"I love you," Danika told Cliona firmly, seeing the relief in her lover's eyes. "But Oli made me realize something and I'm just gonna throw it out there. It's not a deal breaker. I just want you to know where I stand on things."

Silence descended between them, and Danika was quick to try and fill it. "I've spent the last couple of weeks looking at places to call home, and none of them feel right. And Oli made me see it's because you won't be there. So, it's crazy, and probably far too early but move in with me. Let's get a home together. Sell this place or rent it out, but I don't want to get a house that's just mine.

I want to go out and buy our bed. Our sofa. Our goddamn plates and bookshelves and all that domestic crap couples do. I want to come home to you, in our house. I'm in this for the long haul, Cliona. You and me, that's what I want."

Cliona was very quiet for the longest time, and Danika felt her stomach roll. There was no dialing back what she'd just said, what she'd asked Cliona. Danika wanted her to say yes so badly that it physically hurt her to wait Cliona's response.

"You know, when I bought this house from my brother a couple of years ago," Cliona started to say, resting her elbows on the table, her chin in her hands. "I kept telling myself that I'd make the changes I wanted when I had time. But this has always felt like that place I came to hide when my parents threw me away."

Danika leaned back in her chair, and rubbed her sweating palms on her jeans.

"I was stuck in a rut, and maybe a fresh start would be the best thing. I'm not sure how soon we could sell this place, and I don't want to be a kept woman or anything, but I'm in this for the long haul too, Danika. I was gonna ask you to move in here, but there is no security around here or privacy. I'd be worried that some fan might try and break in...that's why I never asked you."

Danika blinked, surprised that Cliona had thought that far ahead. While Danika knew this house wouldn't be sustainable after a while, she would never have turned Cliona down. Letting her excitement show on her face, Danika grinned. "So, in all the places I dragged you to, was there any that you stood in and said, I wouldn't mind shacking up with my rockstar girlfriend here?"

Cliona laughed at Danika, then chewed on her lip. "I did like the view of the city in the penthouse near Rebel Books. And that bathtub was to die for."

"Big enough for two, remember?"

That made Cliona laugh harder, as Danika recalled how she had climbed into the bath and told her that it was big enough for two. Danika had also really liked the open planned layout, as well as the privacy windows, which meant that they could gaze out over the city, but no one could see in. There was also twenty-four-hour security, and an underground car park, and the apartments were soundproof also, so no need to worry about annoying her neighbours if she was testing a new song or making her beautiful girl-friend scream her name.

Oh, she's defo having to test that out.

"You sure?" Danika asked, wanting to make sure she wasn't pressuring Cliona into anything before she was ready.

Cliona blushed, then pulled out her phone and slid it toward her. Danika burst out laughing when she saw Cliona's Ikea wish list, which was cutely titled, C&D's Gaff. Danika set down Cliona's phone, as Cliona told her that they might not be able to afford the penthouse if they were gonna go halves on everything.

Danika pulled out her own phone, then pressed the mobile for the estate agent. "Hey it's Danika Keane. Make an offer on the penthouse off Washington Street. Offer the asking price for a quick sale but let me know if they try to be greedy."

Cliona's mouth hung open. "Dani! You can't just go buy a penthouse like that. There are things that need to be talked about. Lots of things. And I need to sell this place!"

"We can tell the estate agent we have a house to sell when she calls back to tell us the place is ours. Then you and me need a trip to Dublin to start going through your Ikea list. And the penthouse will be ours.

I just have the funds available, so we don't miss out. Let me do this. For us."

Cliona looked worried for a second, then she gave Danika a secret kinda smile. "I get to pay for the bed. I want it right in front of that big window so I can make love to you in the moonlight."

Danika's heart stuttered. She was used to being the one who could write meaningful lyrics, and melodies that stuck with you, but in one simple sentence, Danika fell in love with Cliona all over again.

"Make sure it's sturdy. I've got some fluffy handcuffs we haven't tried out yet."

Chapter Thirty

Cliona

IN THE LAST TEN DAYS, Cliona had learned that it was easier to sell a house than it was to buy a house, even with a rockstar being the one that wanted to buy it. Cliona had met with the estate agent the day after they had made the offer on the penthouse, the house valued and put up for sale, hours later. After a few days, Cliona had an offer and now she was living in Niamh and Oli's house because they were still going back and forth about the penthouse.

Danika was stressed to the nines, what with her label releasing a statement about her not renewing her contract, and the fans going into a meltdown that Danika was quitting music. They had talked it over, and while Cliona was nervous, considering they were shacking up together, as Oli put it, then they really needed to let the fans know why Danika had not signed a new contract with her old label.

Cliona had never seen such a production for one Instagram live. Andrea Collins, PR mogul and fiancé of Declan Walsh was on hand to warn Danika not to go too far off script, and Oli was satisfied that things with the record label were starting to take shape and that Danika could tease that too.

But Cliona was going to be in the video now when Danika explained that she was moving to Ireland to start living her best life. Her heart was in her throat as Andi nodded for Danika to begin.

Dressed in a sleeveless vest and leggings, Danika grinned as the livestream began. "All right, freaks, it's Danika here. I'm enjoying a rare sunny afternoon in Mr. Oliver Scott's back garden but had to come and set the record straight. I'm not leaving music. Just my label. We had creative differences, and it was time to move on. New music is coming in the not-so-distant future."

Andi gave Danika a thumbs up, and Danika continued. "A lot of things have changed in the past couple of months, so I'm gonna share some personal news with you all. I have relocated from London to Ireland, where my best friend has recently set up home because I wanted to be closer to my family. And I'd like to introduce you all to my girlfriend, Cliona, who isn't like us freaks so be nice to her and any shitty comments will get your ass blocked."

Cliona couldn't stop her hands and legs from shaking as she stepped into the frame and Danika immediately wrapped an arm around her waist and grinned even more. "I have also signed an exclusive PR deal with the absolute goddess that is Andrea Collins over at Rebel PR, and me and Oli have some surprises up our sleeves for you all. But for now, I'm gonna go kiss my girl and spend some time with my family. Byee!"

Then it was over, with Andi advising Danika to not check her phone for the afternoon in case she was overwhelmed with the urge to respond to anything bad on social media. Danika had rolled her eyes but put her phone on Do Not Disturb as they enjoyed the sunshine just like Andi had told her to.

The band also came over, and soon enough the garden was packed with rockstars. Andi thought it would be a great idea to post some pics of them all having fun in the sun, to which Danika shouted at Rhys to take off his shirt so his abs could distract all the freaks who were her fans.

Cliona had never seen the striking man look so ruffled.

Didn't stop him from doing just that, and when Danika went to take off her shirt, everyone shouted NO at her, and that made her laugh even more. She posed with Rhys for a few selfies, then dragged Cliona and Shay in for some.

It wasn't long before instruments came out, which

seemed to be their thing. Cliona had commented that it was like a busman's day off, and everyone had given her the dirtiest look. Didn't mean she was wrong.

Niamh went into the house to get some more drinks, and Oli went with her to help. Cliona was sitting down beside Shay, the manager of Rebel Ink and an artist herself. The woman was sketching the band as they messed about and Cliona was watching her work, amazed at the artistry of it all. She had picked up the sharp blue of Danika's eyes, and Cliona knew she'd ask Shay if she would do something for their home, if they managed to close on it that is.

Oli suddenly came rushing out and Cliona darted to her feet, worried something was happening with Niamh. With a shrill whistle, the musicians all stopped as Oli hollered. "Dani, check your goddamn phone!"

Cliona felt a new rush of panic wash over her as Danika yanked her phone out of her pocket, lifted her eyes to Cliona, then hit call on her phone. Walking over to where Danika was standing with a serious face, using her sort of professional voice.

"Okay, yeah. Thank you. I appreciate the call on the weekend." Danika hung up the phone, slid it back into her pocket, and lifted her eyes to Cliona's.

"Hey, what's wrong? Who was that?" Cliona asked, reaching for Danika's hand, her girlfriend giving her hand a little squeeze before she started to explain.

"That was the estate agent," Danika said, and Cliona's heart sank. Of course, they had lost the penthouse. Life was going to fucking perfectly there had to be a spanner thrown in the works.

"And?" Cliona pushed because she needed to hear Danika say it to believe it.

"We got the penthouse."

Cliona was so prepared to talk Danika out of her sadness at not getting the penthouse that she totally missed what Danika had said, letting herself ramble. "Dani, I know that you wanted this place, but we can look for something else and...I'm sorry, what did you just say?"

Danika grabbed her face with her hands and kissed her until she was dizzy. Then they were both bouncing up and down like crazy. Oli brought out some bottles of champagne and then it really was a party. Danika told her that on Monday morning, they had to go in and sign the papers, and although they couldn't move in for a few weeks, but they could start making plans now.

As day turned to night, Oli set a match to the firepit, and they all sat round under the stars, songs were sung, and Cliona felt emotion choke her throat as Danika sang Mary Lambert's *She Keeps Me Warm*, and Cliona couldn't help but think that would be the perfect song to dance to at their wedding. Not that she was planning on proposing or anything...

They had plenty of time to think about marriage and weddings...one day. Just not right now.

Danika and Cliona stayed outside as everyone else

started to head out, and Oli took a very tired Niamh to bed. Then it was just them. Danika got up off her own chair, to sit in front of Cliona, her back against Cliona's chest. Cliona wrapped her arms around Danika.

"Aren't you glad now that you didn't call Nev and Kammie on me? I mean, I always thought I'd end up on the show because someone was pretending to be me, just not because I was accused of pretending to be me."

Cliona smacked her arm, but Danika only tried to wriggle closer, the heat of the fire and her body, making Cliona feel really cosy. "How the hell was I to know? I read a lot of books. Of course, I wasn't gonna believe that Danika motherfucking Keane was interested in little ole me. I'm a nobody."

Danika turned abruptly, looking up at Cliona with those piercing blue eyes. "You are not a nobody, Cliona. Don't even think like that. You are everything to me. I love you."

Danika had said the words to her a dozen times since the first time, and Cliona never tired of hearing it. There was a new conviction in her tone, and maybe this time, Cliona truly believed them. She had never thought herself worthy to be loved, truly and wholly by another person. Though none of them had been Danika.

Cliona had never believed that love could save a person, even after seeing how love had brought

Niamh's brother back to life after years of slowly dying with his grief. And Cliona had been grieving too, in her own way. For love, for acceptance, for family. All the things that she hadn't let herself have in all the years since she had been brave enough to admit who she really was.

And now she had that with Danika and never had I love you sounded so beautiful.

"I love you," Danika repeated, and Cliona kissed her then because sometimes, it took more than words to prove to someone how much you cared about them.

And sometimes, three little words were all one needed.

THE END

The Rebel County Universe Stories continue in Secrets In Ink (Rebel Ink Book 3)

FIND MORE REBEL STORIES ON KINDLE VELLA

Best Laid Plans is the first book in the Rebel Books Trilogy. Rebel Books is part of the Rebel County Universe which will span at least four different businesses, with intersecting timelines, and characters popping up when you least expect them.

THE REBEL RACERS TRILOGY
Available Now:
Adrenaline Junkie (Rebel Racers Book 1)
All or Nothing (Rebel Racers Book 2)
Crash and Burn (Rebel Racers Book 3)

THE REBEL ROCK TRILOGY
Available Now:
Centre Stage (Rebel Rock Book 1)
Strings Attached (Rebel Rock Book 2)
Make or Break (Rebel Rock Book 3)

THE REBEL INK TRILOGY

Available Now:

Breaking the Habit (Rebel Ink Book 1)

Uncomfortably Numb (Rebel Ink Book 2)

Secrets In Ink (Rebel Ink Book 3)

THE REBEL BOOKS TRILOGY

Available Now:

Best Laid Plans (Rebel Books Book 1)

More Than Words (Rebel Books Book 2)

Playlists

Cliona

Cassyette - Behind Closed Doors

Kito - Sad Girl Music (feat. BANKS)

Cassyette - September Rain

LØLØ - u turn me on (but u give me depression)

Gabry Ponte - Dance Dance (feat. Alessandra)

Natalie Jane - AVA

Maisie Peters - Not Another Rockstar

Leah Kate - My Bed

Rain Paris - Bad Romance

FLETCHER - Guess We Lied...

Mae Muller - I Just Came To Dance

Sunlike Brothers - I Kissed A Girl

Mary Lambert - She Keeps Me Warm

Skylar Grey - Love The Way You Lie Part III

As Everything Unfolds – Blossom

Cody Frost - DWYSSWM (Don't Worry Your Secret's Safe with Me)

Paramore - Hello Cold World

Paramore - Hate to See Your Heart Break

Paramore - All I Wanted

RoRo - Ladies

Brooke - That's Rich

biz colletti - Half of You

ALLISTER X - WOW

Billie Marten - I Can't Get My Head Around You

Taylor Swift - All Of The Girls You Loved Before

Shania Twain - Falling - Spotify Singles

Yuna - All I Do

Anna Graceman - Wave

Kina - Can We Kiss Forever?

Chandler Leighton - I THINK YOU TURNED ME

The Pussycat Dolls - Wait A Minute

Aaliyah - Try Again

Demi Lovato - Heart Attack - Rock Version

Halsey - Bad At Love

Cloudy June - Devil Is A Woman

Danika

Pale Waves - Unwanted

Chloe Adams - Dead To Me

Dove Cameron - Girl Like Me

Bea Miller - lonely bitch

Maggie Lindemann - Pretty Girl - Cheat Codes X CADE Remix

Ciara - Like a Boy

girli - I Really F**ked It Up

FLETCHER - Serial Heartbreaker

Leah Kate - Alive and Unwell

DEZI - BAD B!TCH

bludnymph - Lights Out

GALXARA - Go F*ck Myself (GFM)

Chandler Leighton - When You Say My Name

Demi Lovato - EAT ME (feat. Royal & the Serpent)

Lilyisthatyou - Do I make you nervous?

P!nk - So What

Rihanna - ROCKSTAR 101

YONAKA - Rockstar

Ashnikko - You Make Me Sick!

Leikeli47 - Chitty Bang

Bea Miller - cynical

GAYLE - everybody hates me

EMELINE - STRUT

Cloudy June - You Problem

Delilah Bon - I Wish A Bitch Would

BIA - I'M THAT BITCH

Ciara - Da Girls
lozeak - Used To You
P!nk - Just Like a Pill
P!nk - Most Girls
Bea Miller - THAT BITCH
Nelly Furtado - Promiscuous
Ciara - Goodies (feat. Petey Pablo)
Beyoncé - If I Were a Boy
Halsey - I HATE EVERYBODY

ACKNOWLEDGMENTS

None of this would be possible without an amazing team supporting me! Many thanks to:

Publishing House: CTP Publishing
Cover design: Gem Promotions
Interior Formating: Gem Promotions

———

And as always:
Thank you to all the readers!
Whether this is your first book by me or you've been with me for years! I only get to do this because of you, and I am eternally grateful to each and every one of you who took a chance on this Irish author.

About the Author

Susan Harris is a writer from Cork, Ireland and when she's not torturing her readers with heart-wrenching plot twists or killer cliffhangers, she's probably getting some new book related ink, binging her latest TV or music obsession, or with her nose in a book.

Susan LOVES connecting with her fans!
www.susanharrisauthor.com

Also by Susan Harris

The Wings Of Deceit Series

Angel's Gambit, book 1

Angel's Rebel, book 2

The Ever Chace Chronicles

Skin & Bones, book 1

Collateral Damage, book 2

Smoke & Mirrors, book 3

Night of the Hunter, book 4

Never Back Down, book 5

Shortcut to the Grave, book 6

Arsonist's Lullaby, book 7

Of Gods & Monsters, book 8

———

Shattered Memories

———

DEFY THE STARS

A Tale of Two Houses, book 1

Until Death Do Us Part, book 2

In Defiance of the Stars, book 3

Courting Darkness, a novella

THE SANGUINE CROWN

Chaos Theory, book 1

Butterfly Effect, book 2

Wicked Game, book 3

Burn Notice, book 4

Fight Song, book 5

THE SICARIUS SECURITY SERIES

Kiss Of Death, book 1

Leap Of Faith, book 2

Visions Of Destiny, book 3

War Of Hearts, book 4

Flames Of Conflict, book 5

ANTHOLOGY

A Lot Like Christmas